MY LUCKY #13

PIPER RAYNE

Cover Photo: Cover Lab

Cover Design: By Hang Le

1st Line Editor: Joy Editing

2nd Line Editor: My Brother's Editor

Proofreader: My Brother's Editor

About My Lucky #13

Lucky.

The one adjective used to describe my entire hockey career. I prefer to call it hard work, at least I did until my game went to complete crap. I haven't scored in eight games and the team owner is talking about trading me.

I've never believed in superstitions. Never needed one. I suppose I was "lucky" in that way. But now the best way to refer to me is desperate. I'd wear the same socks for an entire year just to be the high-scoring center I used to be.

Imagine my surprise when after spending New Year's Eve with a woman, I score a hat trick in the next game—that's three goals in one game for you non-hockey lovers. Now, I have to track her down and bribe her to do it again before every game. Get your mind out of the gutter, I'm not talking about it.

I find her and when I get to know her better, I end up spending more time thinking about her than my game, but she's made it clear she wants no part of me. She's going to learn that I didn't become a professional hockey player without having to fight for what I want.

My LUCKY #13

CHAPTER 1

"Hey, I heard a rumor about you
and a hot blonde on New Year's Eve."

Aiden

*A*fter a long shower, I throw myself onto my couch and click on the television. I'm greeted by my name coming from the announcer's mouth and I can't switch the channel fast enough. But before I grab the controller, the same old tape from nine games ago plays on the screen. I slide my ass to the edge of the couch as if I haven't seen the exact game-winning goal replayed thousands of times since I fell into the slump of all fucking slumps.

See that guy on the ice? The one who undressed the defenseman and buried the puck in the net? That's me. Nine fucking games ago. Which is the last time I lit the lamp. My teammates rush over to me on screen, patting me on the head, congratulating me. Those were the good days. The happy days. The days I earned my nickname, Shamrock.

Now, I'm down eight games without a goal scored. The trade deadline is creeping up, and the owner has me by the balls.

"I guess we'll see what happens tonight," the sports commentator says. "Maybe something over New Year's changed Drake's luck."

I click off the television and toss the remote onto the sofa cushion. Screw them.

I hate seeing that clip is because it feels like the old me. Even if my game comes back, I won't be that same naïve player who automatically expects to score every game. Up until recently, I was always lucky, could always count on things lining up for me in a game. Hell, that's how I got my nickname in the first place—because I didn't need any of those stupid superstitions the rest of my teammates subscribe to in order to have a good game.

I head to the fridge to make myself a sandwich before the game, repeating the same old mantra in my head that there's no such thing as superstitions. I've never believed in them, and I won't believe in them now.

When that analyst said New Year's, all I thought about was the woman I met at the team owner's New Year's Eve party, Saige. After I spent most of the night with her, she turned out to be my agent's date. Karma at its fucking finest.

All these years traveling and on the road and I finally meet a woman who intrigues me only to discover it can't go anywhere. Because my agent, Joran, is like an older brother. He took me on when some others didn't see my value. He's negotiated all my contracts, gotten me what we both felt I deserved, and stuck his neck out for me more than a few times. No woman is worth fucking up my relationship with my agent.

I eat my sandwich, dress in my suit, and head out to the rink. Because it's just after New Year's, the weather is pretty mild in Florida. I'm not surprised that once I've slid into my high-end SUV and pulled out of my driveway, Joran's name shows up on my Bluetooth screen. He wants to boost me up and act as though he's not fearful that I'm not gonna perform again tonight.

"Hey, Joran," I say.

"Just checking in before the big game." He's obviously in his car too from the amount of road noise in the background.

"I'm good. On my way to the rink now."

"Awesome. Listen, I wanted to tell you this story I just heard from an agent at our firm."

"What story?" I entertain him because, well, I'm out of ideas on how to get out of this slump. Desperate times and all.

"He said he had a client once who kept striking out at the plate."

"Baseball?"

"Just listen to me, okay?"

"Okay." I'm already tuning him out as I signal to make a right turn.

"Finally mid-season, all the announcers are talking about him and the team GM is calling him into the office. They're reworking his swing, calling in other hitting coaches. Nothing works."

"Is this supposed to be an uplifting story?" I brake when some idiot changes lanes and cuts me off.

Joran chuckles. "Hold on. I'm getting there."

I change lanes and give the guy the finger when I pull up beside him at a red light. Of course he pretends not to see me, his vision focused straight ahead.

"He saw a shrink and voilà, some deep shit from his childhood came up. Once he got it all out and made amends, he hit a two-run homer the next game."

My shoulders sink. I don't have any childhood shit to deal with. I have parents who, if anything, almost put themselves in the poorhouse for me to pursue a career in hockey. I didn't have a pro father who worked me tirelessly until perfection. My parents hired coaches and sought out the best teams for me.

"Well, I don't think that's my problem." I slam down on the gas when the light changes, then return the favor to the jerk by cutting him off the same way he did me.

"That was my way of telling you that Gerhardt wants you to see one. In fact, he's hired a shrink for the entire team and you're first on the list."

"Seriously, a psychologist?" Talking about the stress I'm under because I haven't scored isn't going to get the puck in the net.

"Gerhardt thinks it's the golden ticket," he says.

Gerhardt is Carl Gerhardt, owner of Florida Fury and ultimately my boss. I can't really say no to his request for me to see a psychologist, but I'm not sure what we're gonna talk about. Unless they're some miracle worker with voodoo magic they can sprinkle on me, I'm pretty sure this is gonna be a waste of time. My game is absolutely pathetic these days.

"Fine. When do I have to see her or him?"

"It's a her, and you'll see her tomorrow. Unless you can make magic happen tonight. Hey, I heard a rumor about you and a hot blonde on New Year's Eve."

This is how out of touch Joran is with what's happening around him. During the party, he was so consumed with schmoozing that he didn't know where his date was and has no idea that the hot blonde he's referring to was his date.

"It was nothing."

"Did you get a good-night kiss? Maybe that's the lucky charm you need? Getting laid on the regular does amazing things for an athlete's games."

He's not wrong, but I think sex can do one of two things to an athlete—either become a distraction or help them get rid of the pressure. I haven't had a serious relationship since I entered the NHL. Too many puck bunnies hanging around locker rooms to trust that they want me and not my paycheck. The women I see never last longer than a few dates and that's always been in the off-season.

"No good-night kiss." I'm too embarrassed to say that I went in for a kiss and got a drink thrown in my face.

The memory flashes back through my mind.

"So what do you say? Can I kiss you?" I leaned in, millimeters from her beautiful face, and she closed her eyes as the guy with the microphone announces two… one.

Just as I was about to make contact with her delicious lips, a splash of white wine landed on my face.

I backed away and wiped my face. "What the hell?"

"I'm sorry. I can't." She walked away and up the outside staircase of the mansion.

Shortly after, I found out she was there with Joran—when he introduced me to his date, the same woman I'd been flirting with all evening.

"Listen, I need to play some pregame music and get in the zone. I'll talk to you after the game." My thumb hovers over the *End Call* button on my steering wheel.

"Yeah, of course. I'll be watching and no pressure, Aiden, you're gonna get out of this."

"Talk to you later, Joran." I hang up and let my favorite song, "'Til I Collapse" by Eminem, filter through the SUV, hoping it will drown out all the doubt.

*F*our hours later.

"Holy fuck!" Maksim opens a bottle of champagne and sprays it over the entire locker room.

You'd think we just won the Cup.

"I bought this on the way here today. I knew today was your day." He dumps the bottle over my head while I grin.

Ford slaps me on the back. "A fucking hat trick. You're a damn beast." He opens his mouth and Maksim pours some champagne down Ford's throat.

The entire team is all smiles and cheers. I sit in the locker room while everyone's talking about the big power move, our goalie's shutdowns, and my blast from the point. Nothing has felt better in a long damn time.

"What did you do? Taco Bell? Socks? You look like you got a haircut," my teammate, Tweetie, asks from across the room. "What's the new superstition? Because I speak for all of us when I say that we'll make whatever it is happen for you."

I rack my brain, thinking about what I did differently between this game and our last one before New Year's Eve. I wasn't lying when I told Saige on New Year's Eve that I've never really had superstitions. Never before now. But I need to keep this momentum going, so I think about my breakfast, my lunch, and my dinner. Same things I've had before any other game. I got to the rink at the same time as normal. All my clothes have been freshly laundered.

"Did you get some? Because isn't that girl the lucky chick. She's got you for the entire season." Ford unlaces his skates, and I shake my head before something else clicks in my brain.

I'm pretty sure no one's superstition has ever been crashing and burning while hitting on a woman.

"DRAKE!" Coach Vittner calls from his office.

I slip on my slides and walk across the room still in my pads. My teammates are all patting me on the back for a great job. It's one of the best things about being on a team when you do things that boost everyone.

"Yeah, Coach?" I peek my head in and he gestures me to come inside.

"Close the door. You guys are way too loud tonight." But he's smiling and I catch an open bottle of Jack Daniels on his desk. Looks like even the coach is celebrating. "Good game tonight. I'm proud of you. Whatever you did, you need to fucking repeat it for the next game."

"I didn't do anything differently and I don't really believe in superstitions—"

"You're a hockey player."

Okay, I should clarify it's not that I don't believe in superstitions, I've just never needed them. I guess I'm new to the whole obsession.

"I just wanted to call you in here because you played great tonight. I got wind of what could be gossip, but if your performance doesn't stay like it was tonight, there's a chance your bags are packed by the end of February."

"Trade?"

He sighs. "If it was my decision, it's a no-brainer. I knew you'd be where you are tonight. But it's the big man. He makes the decisions. Let's give it to him right in the ass for even thinking of getting rid of you."

I fucking love Coach Vittner, and this is why. He's a true leader and goes to bat for his players all the damn time.

"Shit. Just as the pressure was easing up."

He chuckles. "I tell you this to encourage you to do everything in your power to score and win, not to make you depressed like some teenage boy who hasn't touched his first tit. Come on, Drake. You've got this."

"But what if next game I don't?" Even I hate the unsureness in my tone.

"Oh fuck, that's not what I wanna hear. I wanna hear

you say you're gonna score. You're gonna win. You're gonna screw Carl Gerhardt right up the ass."

"Well…" I cock my head.

"Too far, I know. But go out there and celebrate tonight. And whatever you did before tonight's game, repeat it."

"Yes, sir." I turn, and with my hand on the doorknob, I stop. "Coach?" I turn back and he's drinking his Jack Daniels from a paper cup. "The whole superstition thing is like twenty-four hours before game time?"

He shrugs. "Every hockey player has their own. I guess you're about to find out what yours is. But don't go experimenting and fuck it up. Anything that's different in your life, do before next game."

"But—"

"Drake, we're not building a damn rocket here. If this is about some girl you slept with last night, hate to break it to you, but retrieve that phone number out of the trash. We're talking about your career here."

I nod and leave Coach's office.

Maksim comes up to me, naked, swinging his huge dick way too close to me. "What do you need me to do? Pick up food from a certain place? Not touch your shit? Wear your jockstrap? Hell, you name it."

"Yeah, Shamrock, we're your men. Whatever you need us to do to make this a streak." Ford comes alongside Maksim, looking down. "Goddamn, remind me never to do a porno with you."

I think long and hard. "I think I have to track someone down. Maksim, do you have a business card from that woman we met on New Year's—Saige?"

"The cute blonde?" he asks.

"I knew you went home with her when we couldn't find you. Home alone, my ass." Ford flips me off.

"Yeah, the blonde." I nod at Maksim.

He reaches into his bag and hands it to me. "Here you go."

I sit on the bench and twirl the card around in my hands. I have to be delusional to be thinking she has anything to do with my performance on the ice tonight, right? But why risk it?

I shove the card into my bag and hit the showers. My career is everything and I need to protect it. I have to keep this up, no matter the cost.

Saige

"Good morning," I say to my assistant, Tedi.

She glances up and blows a strand of her dark hair away from her face. "There's nothing good about the morning."

I drop a pastry bag on her desk and her eyes light up. "Unless there's a chocolate croissant in there." I smile at her before walking past her desk, and I hear her open up the bag to discover that there is, in fact, a chocolate croissant for her. "Oh, I love you."

Our office is small, but we tried to work out of my apartment, and I kept finding her on the couch, watching reality television and saying she's a great multi-tasker. Not that all the blame is on her—she'd suck me in and then I'd start doing my client's social media from the couch in my pajamas.

She takes the croissant out of the bag and stares at it as if it's a naked Chippendale dancer. "Come to mama!" She takes a huge bite.

I giggle and set my coffee on the desk before shrugging out of my jacket. Although we're in Florida, it's winter. There may not be snow, but it's freezing outside. You'd never guess I'm originally an Idaho girl.

"How was your night?" I ask.

"Good. How was your date with Joran on New Year's Eve?"

I sit down in my chair and pick up a pen, teetering it back and forth.

Tedi groans. "I don't understand why you're still dating him."

"Because he's the most decent guy since…"

"Asshole. Repeat after me… Ass. Hole."

"I don't want to talk about Jeremy."

She throws her arms in the air. "Now you've ruined my day. You know I can't stand his name."

"He's *my* ex."

"Yes, but I had to endure him all the same."

"It's been two years," I remind her.

Tedi was our neighbor when I moved down here to Florida with Jeremy. She's the one who told me about him cheating when I went to work, and we've been best friends ever since.

"Anyway, I'm not sure how much longer it'll last with Joran." I speak honestly because I tell Tedi everything, although I haven't told her about my encounter with Aiden Drake. Mostly because she's a hockey fanatic and would make a bigger deal out of it than it is. When Joran had invited me to the New Year's party, I wasn't even sure if anyone from the team would be attending. I just knew it would be a bunch of rich people out of my league if they were invited by the Gerhardts.

She leans her chair back and crosses her ankles on the edge of the desk. "What happened?" she mumbles around her croissant.

"New Year's was kind of a bust and the other night, I went to the Fury game with him."

"Seriously? And you didn't invite me?"

"I was in a box with him and people from his office. I

spent most of the game watching it on my own, even
though I don't know much about hockey. Joran said there
was some rookie kid in the box he wanted to impress. I
honestly wondered why he even brought me in the first
place."

"I could've been your tutor," she says.

"You've tried, remember? I'll never understand why
they come and go off the bench so much and what it all
means."

She laughs. "For someone who does social media for
athletes, you might wanna try harder."

I stick out my tongue at her and she laughs.

"Watch out, your face might freeze like that."

"Anyway. Aiden—"

"Drake?" Her eyes light up. "He's out of his funk. Did
you hear?" She twirls in her chair. "He had an amazing
game."

I watched from the box, elated for a man I barely
know. Joran might as well have orgasmed by the third goal,
screaming so loud that families below the box were staring
at us. I can't deny that after I got home and turned on the
television, I listened to the announcers talk about his
slump, showing pictures of the amazingly strong man's
head hung in defeat after so many other bad games, a huge
smile pulled on my face that he'd finally scored again. Not
only once, but three times in one game.

"Saige?" Tedi says with a tone of curiosity.

I snap back to the present. "Yeah?"

She circles her finger in front of my face. "That."

I wipe at my face with my hand. I scarfed down a
muffin on the way here and must've left some evidence
behind.

"There's nothing on your face except that you look like
you just woke up from one helluva wet dream."

"Tedi," I groan.

She laughs and finishes her croissant, grabbing the coffee she brought from home in her Go Florida Fury travel mug. I will say that after seeing a game like the one last night, I see why people like hockey. It's fast-paced, and when someone scores, the screams from the fans are contagious.

"I told you, those hockey players are hot. I love it when they fight." Her gaze drifts up to the ceiling as if she's in a dream-like state.

I roll my eyes. There's no denying they're attractive. Aiden especially. He has these eyes I swear see into your soul. Dark and dangerous. "I'm not sure I love the fighting."

"Oh my god, you're crazy. You know Maksim Petrov? He's a defender."

I nod. I'm supposed to have a meeting with Maksim tomorrow, and I'm thinking an off-site meeting might be better so Tedi doesn't try to climb him like a tree.

We're mid-conversation when our office door opens. Because we're appointment only, we rarely get drop-ins except the mail carrier, so I'm shocked to find Aiden Drake standing there. He walks in, passes Tedi's open mouth, and comes over to me, placing a wine glass and a bottle of white wine on my desk.

"Aiden," I say, sliding my desk chair back.

He doesn't sugarcoat his reason for being here. "I need you to throw this drink in my face."

I stare at him with surprise, then amusement. He's got to be kidding me.

"Listen." He looks back at Tedi—who I'm shocked hasn't chimed in, then grabs the chair from in front of my desk and sits on the edge of it, leaning forward and placing his forearms on my desk.

Yep, still drool-worthy.

"I told you how I was in a slump on New Year's Eve, right?"

"Oh, you dirty little——"

I raise my hand to stop Tedi from continuing. Aiden glances over his shoulder for a second before returning his attention to me.

"Well, my last game was killer. Three goals plus an assist. And…" He glances over his shoulder again. Tedi's staring at him as if he's her second chocolate croissant for the day. "Could we go somewhere private?"

Tedi narrows her eyes at me. "Oh, you're in so much trouble."

"It's okay. Tedi knows whatever happens in here is private. Tedi, this is Aiden Drake."

She gets up from her chair and comes over, hand out. To my surprise, Aiden doesn't check her out the way I thought he might—Tedi's very attractive. I haven't found the nerve to Google Aiden yet—because I don't want to find out he's a womanizer and that on New Year's Eve, I was just the girl who happened to be the one he thought he'd get into his bed for the night.

"I'm Tedi, president of your fan club," she says, shaking his hand and staring at his much larger one. "Whoa, the damage you could do to a little thing like me with hands like those."

"Tedi," I sigh.

She laughs. "I'm totally joking. You're not my type at all."

Aiden's eyebrows haven't come down from being raised to his hairline yet. He glances at me then back at Tedi. "That's good… I think."

"You actually believed that?" She laughs and smacks him on the shoulder. "You're everyone's type, my man. I mean, center on a professional hockey team, team captain, chiseled jaw, dark hair, and those eyes. They always look like something filthy is going on behind them."

I want to high-five Tedi—his eyes are exactly what drew me to him. It was like he was undressing me with his eyes and envisioning what he would do to me if we were alone.

Aiden nods. "Thanks?"

"You're welcome. I don't mind boosting a guy's ego once in a while, but don't hurt my best friend here. Ask her what happened to the other guy who hurt her." Tedi's tone grows serious, and her face actually makes her threat believable. Though other than helping me toss Jeremy's clothes over the balcony, I'm not sure I remember anything else she did to him.

He raises his hand. "I'm only here for her to throw a drink in my face."

"Which I'm not going to do," I chime in and earn his attention. Big mistake having those dark eyes on me again.

His shoulders fall. "You have to. If you don't, I won't be able to score tonight."

I laugh. I understand superstitions—I've had my own throughout my life—but this is way out there. "I thought you didn't believe in superstitions?"

Tedi grabs her chair and wheels it over, getting comfortable, sitting with her legs crossed.

Aiden looks from her back to me. "I didn't until that game. Everything about my life was normal until the night we met."

"You should've slept with him. Imagine what would've happened then," Tedi says.

"I'm going to put duct tape across your mouth if you don't stop talking," I warn her.

She raises her hands, smiling. "I'm just saying, then

you'd have to sleep with him before every game. I bet you're good in bed. I mean all that training… the stamina you must have."

Aiden's mouth opens and shuts as though he has no idea how he should answer. "I do all right."

Even I know he could probably press me to a wall and fuck my brains out until he had no choice but to lay me down to recuperate.

Tedi laughs and says nothing.

"The drink in the face means nothing," I say, hoping to end this.

"What do you want in return? Season tickets? Done."

"I don't watch hockey."

Tedi raises her hand. "I'll do it for season tickets. I'm your biggest fan."

"Clothes? A shopping spree?" he asks.

I cross my legs. "You're not going to buy me anything. I'm not looking for a sugar daddy."

"I'll give you anything, just name it. A date with me?" He winks.

I hope he's joking. "Let's remember, I'm kind of dating your agent."

His smile falters. "Come on. I'm begging. Do you want me down on my knees?" He moves to stand, and I put up my hand.

"I'll gladly go down on my knees for the season tickets."

"*Tedi!*" I screech.

She knows me well and can see I've reached my limit, so she stands and wheels her chair away. "I'll just go mind my business over here. But I gotta say, you might as well experiment. See if it works this time. Maybe it was a fluke, but you won't know until you do it another time."

I narrow my eyes at her while Aiden points at her. "She has a point."

I groan and put my head on my desk. Why am I really arguing this? He's not asking for anything more than a drink in the face.

"Fine." I pick up my head, grab the bottle, and pour a glass.

"Really?" Aiden stands. "Should we mimic the way we were standing?"

"How were you standing?" Tedi asks as if it's a juicy piece of gossip.

"I don't think that's necessary," I say, picking up the glass and tossing the wine in his face.

His eyes widen in shock and his tongue slides out and licks his lips. "I'm not much of a wine guy, but I'm starting to enjoy the sweetness." He winks. "I've got a game in two nights. I'll be back." He grabs a piece of paper and scribbles down his number, pushing it my way. "That's my number if you need me."

I stare at it for a moment, then catch Tedi's eyes widening, her mouth ajar.

"Thanks, Saige. This means a lot to me."

His sincerity hits me right in the chest and a warm feeling radiates outward.

"I'll put two tickets at will call under your name for tonight." He picks up one of my business cards and twirls it in his fingers. "And remember when I shoot that goal, it's all because of you."

Then he's out the door. I slump back into my office chair to calm my breathing.

"Oh yeah, I can totally see that you're not interested in that guy," Tedi says, shaking her head.

I have to tread carefully here because Tedi's right. But things could get out of control fast with a man like Aiden

Drake, and I swore a long time ago that I'd never date a professional athlete again.

Been there.

Done that.

Shattered heart to prove it.

CHAPTER 3

"She's not a damn puck bunny."

Aiden

"So tell me you did her?" Ford asks the minute I step foot in the locker room.

I narrow my eyes. "I have no idea what you're talking about."

"The blonde. New Year's Eve." He undoes his tie, following me to my locker. "You nailed her, right? So we should expect Shamrock on the ice again tonight?"

Ford means well, he really does. He's just spoiled and lives a privileged life. But I have no doubt the day is coming when some woman will get him on his knees, begging.

"No, it's not like that."

Despite me assuring them I slept alone after the party, my teammates think I ghosted them on New Year's Eve because I was getting laid. In their minds, I slept with Saige, and so in order for me to have another great game tonight, I have to sleep with her again.

"Let's just say it's taken care of," I say like a fucking weasel. I feel like I'm back in high school, except I never had time for girls in high school because I was always training and working on my game. But I don't want to lie about Saige and me. She's no puck bunny, that's for sure. "But I didn't sleep with her."

"Sure, you didn't." Ford pats me on the back, practically jumping up as we enter the changing area. "No worries, guys, our captain did his duty!"

A roar of applause and shouts ring out from everyone.

I shake my head and sit in front of my locker.

Maksim joins me on my other side. "I'm so fucking excited for tonight now." He unclasps his slacks. "We're gonna kick the Sharks' ass," he says in his Russian accent.

Another roar from our team. Everyone is in good spirits. I don't think that telling them that the superstition might be a woman throwing white wine at my face will crumble their spirit, so I promise myself I'll tell them after the game. Definitely after we come back with a win. Of course, if I don't score, then it was all for nothing anyway and my last game was just a coincidence.

Ford gets everyone hyped up, playing his hip-hop, and dancing as he changes into his gear. The man loves to party. I keep to myself and change into my pads.

"Did you hear? I hired the blonde yesterday," Maksim says, lacing up his skates.

"For your social media?"

He nods and smiles. "I hate that shit. I can't stand seeing all the shitty comments. Messes with my head."

"You could forgo social media," I tell him, and he balks.

"You might get away with that because you're Aiden Drake, but for a lot of us, it's how we gain fans and get sponsorships."

"But now the blonde is doing your posting." I quirk an eyebrow.

He laughs. "True, but she said I could post anything as long as I clear it with her. She gave me some great tips on how to keep stalkers away. She's gonna be like my fairy godmother. Well, a hot fairy godmother."

Hot indeed.

"One day, you'll have to get back on social media."

I shake my head. "Never gonna happen, my friend. I'm off the grid when it comes to shit like that."

I had accounts until… I stop myself from going down that line of thought.

"I guess it doesn't matter since you've got the hot blonde in your bed."

"I told you..." I run my hand through my hair. "I didn't sleep with her."

"Yeah right."

"She's dating Joran. I *can't* sleep with her."

His ass falls to the bench and he looks as if I just told him his puppy got run over by a semitruck. "But you said—"

"I said I took care of it and I did."

"How?" His blue eyes look weepy.

I blow out a breath, but I know I can trust Maksim with this. He's been there for me during my entire slump, staying in my ear about the hotshot I am. "Just trust me, okay?"

His eyebrows raise to his hairline. "So she blew you?"

My head falls back. "No. Nothing sexual. She's dating Joran, remember?"

His head shakes. "I trust you, but if you don't come out on top tonight, I'm thinking maybe you should nail her." He stands on his skates. "I gotta use the can."

"Should've done that before you put on your skates!" Ford yells and sits down next to me.

"It's his superstition," I remind Ford.

He laughs. "I know, but seriously, it's just gross."

I laugh and lace up my own skates. At least Maksim puts on new guards afterward. I eye our poor water boy, Tyler, waiting with the new pair.

"Did you hear about the therapist old Gerhardt hired?" Ford asks.

I nod.

"I told Coach I've seen enough therapists in my life. I don't need one to play hockey."

"You need someone to stop you from doing stupid shit like getting in a bar fight." Being captain, I have to say it how it is. Not that any other teammate wouldn't tell him the same. He's like a wild dog—hard to put a collar on, let alone a leash.

"Come on. The guy asked for it."

"We have a reputation. We don't want to be the team who starts fights off the ice."

He holds up his hands. "Did Lena get a hold of you or something?"

Lena is Ford's family's PR rep, and by now, we've all seen a time or two when she's called to give him hell about something or other that's been in the press. I've yet to bring up the rumor I heard about Ford sneaking out of the New Year's Eve party and flying back to New York with her. If anyone wants to put him on a leash, it's his father, but he relies on Lena to do it. Too bad she's yet to figure out Ford.

"Come on. You don't want that reputation. You have a lot more years in hockey."

He finishes lacing up his skates. "Well, I plan on having my therapist write a letter to Gerhardt to say I can't be counseled by two people, it'll just mess me up even more." He grins as if his plan is brilliant.

I shake my head as he walks away.

Maksim comes out of the bathroom and switches out his guards before walking out to the hallway.

I grab my helmet, gloves, and stick and head out of the locker room. All the guys are roaring and screaming, patting me on the head since I go out on the ice last. They go through the announcing of players and when my name is called, the second my skates hit the ice, the cool air rushes up my nostrils—my body calms. The best feeling in the world is when I push off on my skates and glide with my stick out in front of me.

I circle around on our side of the ice and give a wave to the crowd, then take my spot. My eyes search for the seats I left the tickets for. They're both empty and I shake my head. I hoped Saige would come tonight. She's Joran's girl and I have to remember that. At least he's not here, since he had to go smooth over another client's situation. When he comes to games, more times than not, he ends up in the locker room. Drives Coach crazy.

They do all the pregame bullshit as always then sing the national anthem and as soon as the final note stops we all start our warmup skate. I get the puck and slap shot it into the net past our goalie. There's a crowd of people waving at me and I tap the end of my stick on the glass.

Halfway through our drills, Ford finds it funny to moonwalk past the fans. They all scream and wave, putting him up on the Jumbotron. The guy will do anything for attention. But if he hadn't done that, I wouldn't have seen Saige coming down the stairs with her friend, an usher directing them to the front row.

Fuck me because I know I'm smiling a little too wide for a girl who's not mine.

Ford skids to a stop. "You gave your puck bunny front row seats?"

"She's not a damn puck bunny."

"What would you call her then?" He skates off before I can answer.

I wish I knew.

Tedi spots me and waves. She comes to the glass with a sign that says she's single and has her phone number on it.

Saige joins her, looks at the sign, and tears it out of her hands with a pissed-off look.

I skate by and nod at them, watching Saige as I pass. Tedi frantically waves and elbows the man next to her, pointing at me.

This is my favorite part of the game. The anticipation in the air while the arena is filling up. You can feel the excitement coming off the fans as we get closer to the start time. We all feed off that adrenaline.

Most of the team files onto the bench, but I stay out on the ice with Maksim and Ford and the other guys since we're on the first line.

"Goddamn, I hate that fucking prick," Ford says, his eyes on the Sharks across the way.

"Whatever beef you have with him, you guys need to end it. I'm not fighting your battles this time," Maksim says.

We all know that as soon as Ford and Warner Langley set eyes on one another, it isn't gonna be good. I don't know the entire story, but they came up together in the same league and some fight happened that turned them from best friends to enemies. Every time we play the Sharks, it's hard to keep Ford on task. It doesn't help that Warner is one of the best left wingers in the league.

"Don't go acting like you slam him into the wall on account of me. His chirping gets under your skin too." Ford shakes his head, securing his helmet.

"Let's just worry about winning, okay?" I put my gloved hands up in front of both of them.

"Hey, you three monkeys want in on the play, or are we gonna talk about the cute boy in English class?" Coach yells at us.

The three of us skate forward to see his play. Once we're all on the same page, and the national anthem is sung and the rest of the pregame crap is out of the way, it's game time. My fist clenches as I skate to the red line at center ice.

"Ready to get your ass kicked?" Warner Langley says across the line to Ford.

"In your fucking dreams. Everyone knows we're the better team," Ford says.

"Until your center turned into a head case," Warner says, making me turn my head and lose the fucking drop.

"Told you why I fucking hate the guy," Ford shouts while we both skate like hell toward the puck.

"Maksim, take him to the board every chance you get!" I yell.

I don't need acknowledgment from him. He'll do it.

I try to gain control of the puck from the Sharks' center. I can't believe I lost the drop. Fucking Langley.

The crowd is in an uproar and I slide my stick in, miraculously stealing the puck and passing it to Ford. He takes control and I skate like hell to reach him. When he gets cornered, he shoots it to our left winger, Tweetie, and he gets it to me right by the net. All I have to do is practically tap it in. I do my signature celebratory goal move, but as I pop back up, my gaze is on Saige.

Her attention is on her phone, but Tedi's jumping up and down.

"Looks like the hot blonde did the trick again," Ford says, patting me on the back, and skates off.

Is it bad that I would've liked her to see me score? It's not the best sign since she's my agent's girl.

CHAPTER 4

"Oh my god, it's so hot. Like cavemen."

Saige

 edi elbows me in the breast. "Did you see that? He scored!" She flies out of her seat and bangs on the glass.

I peek up from my phone to see Aiden staring at us. God, he's so sexy. What the hell am I doing here? Men like Aiden are my kryptonite.

After another player bangs his stick on the boards, and Tedi collapses back in her seat. "Did you see that? That was Tweetie." She's talking to the guy sitting next to her even though I think he's a Sharks' fan since he's wearing blue and silver while she's decked out in the Fury colors of black and white.

"How do you know so much about hockey?" I ask her.

"I have brothers. They played. They weren't very good, since they're both architects now." She sits up straighter in her chair. "They weren't tough enough."

"Oh," is all I say.

"I guess that white wine did the trick, huh?"

I eye her because I'm sure Aiden doesn't want anyone to know about some weird superstition he has now. Plus, since he scored a goal, I'm fairly sure he's going to be on my doorstep before his next game.

My phone rings and I see my biggest client, Maverick

Sanders's, name on the screen. He's a pro football player for the Miami team and was my first client who trusted me fully. Handed me his entire social media, including a webpage. So no matter where I am, Maverick always gets his phone call answered.

"Hey, Maverick," I say, pushing one finger to my ear.

"Where are you?" he asks.

"I'm at the Fury game."

"What? All the times I've tried to get you to my games, you said you don't enjoy sports."

It's true. Maverick has offered me killer seats, and I always decline. Games are a dangerous place for me. Because of my work, I get to go behind the scenes and associate with the players. I understand the appeal a pro athlete has on my libido and I don't take chances, since most of them are only interested in one thing and usually only for one night. The only reason I'm here tonight is because Tedi played a major guilt trip on me.

"Sorry, nothing personal."

"You're fired!" he says and laughs.

My gut twists. Maverick is the cornerstone of my entire business. He's the face on every piece of marketing material I have. Just the use of his name gets me other athletes as clients. If I lose him, I'm screwed.

"What?" I ask, the lump in my throat growing bigger.

He laughs again and my shoulders relax a bit. Okay, he really is joking. "I was kidding when I said that, but the truth is that I do have to fire you."

"I'm sorry?" I stand and shuffle down the row before walking up the stairs of the arena.

"Yeah, you know how Emery and I just got engaged?"

"Yes." I know because she's been sending me pictures of them to post, wanting me to report every time they're doing anything from grocery shopping to a date night to a fundraiser. I keep telling her they should keep some things private and never post live, always post after they've left, but she never listens to me.

"She's going to take it over."

"Maverick," I say with displeasure in my tone because this is the stupidest decision ever. If he wanted to try it on his own, then have at it, but not his girlfriend. There's no way she has his best interests at heart.

"She's got the time, and honestly, she really wants to do it."

I can almost hear Emery's whiny voice pleading with Maverick.

"I really don't think it's a good idea. She's too close, too personal. Remember when I first took it over for you because people were ambushing you when you were out socially?"

"She promised me she wouldn't do that again."

I'm silent for a moment because this is a huge blow. I'll have to redo my entire marketing campaign. "Have you really thought this through?"

"It's social media. How bad can she screw it up?"

My back straightens. I'm annoyed that he thinks my job is nothing but a joke. Does he have any idea how many more followers I've gotten him, or that he doesn't come off like a privileged, condescending asshole now? Has he added up all the money he's gotten from the partnering posts I've secured on his behalf? "Okay, I'll send over a document to cancel our contract first thing in the morning and provide you with all the passwords. As long as you're sure."

"I'm sure she'll do fine."

"Sure, she will."

Not. Definitely not. She's going to make a mess of it. I've shown their relationship a bit, but the women who follow Maverick don't want to hear about Emery. That's why it's all going to blow up in his face.

"Thanks for understanding, Saige."

"Good luck," I say and hang up.

I stand by the concession booth, staring at the large pretzel covered in salt. My bruised ego tells me that will fix my problem. Without thinking of much else, I buy the pretzel and cheese and a large beer.

When I walk down the stairs toward the first row, there's a frenzy of hockey players whizzing by on skates, and I grow nauseated.

Tedi eyes me for a moment. "Who was that?"

I tear off a piece of the pretzel and dip it into the cheese. "Maverick," I say as if it's no big deal.

I think I'm still in shock. I didn't see this coming. We were great business associates. He was so helpful in the beginning, always referring me to people. I thought he saw my value, but to just hand it over to his fiancée and say it's no big deal? He clearly didn't.

"And?" Tedi pulls a piece of my pretzel off for herself.

"He's no longer with Stars SM."

Tedi's mouth opens but nothing comes out.

I nod to confirm she heard me right, and she plunges her pretzel piece into the cheese, sitting straight and staring at the ice, unblinking.

"Asshole," she mumbles.

I don't agree or disagree. I don't know what to think. Just when I was starting to feel secure about my business, this happens. I spent a huge amount on the marketing materials I just had made, which I'll now have to scrap. Add on the fact that when a high-profile client leaves, it can fill those who are still with the business or thinking about coming on board with doubt. I swear, every time my life gets better, I'm thrown another wrench to dodge.

"No worries though, because look at all these guys who need social media taken off their hands." Tedi wraps her arm around me and motions toward the ice.

"True. I have Maksim poised to sign on."

"Yeah, he's a hot Russian for sure, but you need more than him to replace Maverick."

She's right. I'd need about six of them or… I shake my head. The only player on that ice who would be on par with Maverick is Aiden Drake. He's the captain of the team. And although I pretended not to know who he was on New Year's Eve, did he really think I don't know every athlete who's worth knowing?

But it shows you my weakness that I allowed him to spend time with me and corner me. I had been milliseconds away from him kissing me before I remembered I don't date athletes. My reason should have been Joran, but I'm not really his girlfriend.

The first period ends, and I feel ready to just go home at this point. I'm annoyed by everything.

A boy around thirteen or so heads down the stairs and approaches us. He's dressed in head-to-toe Fury gear.

"Saige?" he asks, holding out a piece of paper.

I don't say anything because I'm skeptical about why this kid knows my name and wants to hand me a note.

"I'll take that, kid." Tedi snags it out of his hand.

"Are you Saige? I was told it was for her only."

I lean forward to look at the bench and see Ford Jacobs wink. Now there's a man who could use someone to clean up his image online.

"Did Ford Jacobs tell you to give this to her?" Tedi asks.

"So you aren't Saige?" The kid takes the note out of her hand and holds it out to me. "Please? He gives the meanest noogies."

I smile at the kid and accept the note, just thankful it's not from Aiden. "Thanks."

He jogs back up the stairs and disappears.

"Well, open it." Tedi nudges me with her bony elbow.

I put my beer in the cup holder and unfold the piece of paper. The note-passing has earned me some attention from nearby fans. The woman next to me is pretending not to be leaning over to read what it says.

All that's written there is, *Carmelo's* after the game.

I pass it to Tedi, and she squeals. "We're going, right?"

I shake my head.

"Come on," Tedi whines, almost in full-on toddler tantrum mode.

"Why?"

"Hello, I know you've been glued to your phone and ignoring all the hot guys on the ice in front of us, but Tweetie keeps giving me the eye and do you want to be the reason I can't scratch sleeping with a hockey player off my fuck-it bucket list?"

"I thought you scratched that off your list two years ago."

She stops and looks at the ceiling. "Oh." She nods. "But he was in the AHL. That doesn't count."

I blow out a breath. Tedi and her fuck-it bucket list. But she does a lot for me for not the best salary, so if I have to endure a bunch of hockey players for a few hours so she can get laid by one of them, so be it. "Fine."

"Seriously? I thought for sure this would be one of those times you put your foot down."

"It's fine, but once it looks like you don't need me, I'm out, okay?"

She leans forward and down toward the penalty box where Tweetie currently is, smiling and waving as if she's some sweet innocent girl. She'll be hanging from his rafters if he takes her home tonight.

I'm distracted by a body slamming into the boards, and I'm shocked when I glance up to see Aiden is the one who did the slamming. The other guy shakes off his gloves, and Aiden does the same. They circle one another once, then both grab the other's jersey and fists fly. The refs eventually skate in between, trying to stop them.

"Oh my god, it's so hot. Like cavemen." Tedi tears off a piece of my pretzel again. I'm not even hungry anymore, so I hand her the entire thing, concentrating on my beer.

Tedi's right though. I want to tear my gaze from the brawl, but I can't find the willpower. Aiden gets pulled off the guy he shoved into the boards and his lip is bleeding, along with a spot right above his eyebrow. Somehow, it only adds to his sex appeal. Damn it all to hell.

CHAPTER 5

*"You're not the first one to improve
a man's game that way."*

Aiden

*W*hen Maksim and I walk into Carmelo's, the entire bar explodes into a cheer of "Lucky 13, Lucky 13!"

Maksim slaps me on the back. "Yeah, man, you're back."

It feels fantastic to actually be contributing again with some goals and assists. Especially tonight, when we were tied one-one and only twenty seconds left on the clock. Ford passed me the puck, and fucking Langley thought he had me with his fancy footwork and shit, but I passed it to Tweetie. Ford went in and took Langley to the boards, Tweetie passed back to me, and I slap shot the goal in from the far right with barely an opening in the net.

At the next face-off, the Sharks tried but failed at getting it past our goalie, Trigger. The only shitty part is that I wanted to see Saige to tell her thanks for doing me a solid with the drink in my face, but by the time I got out of the huddle with the guys and skated over to where she was sitting, she and her friend were already walking up the stairs.

After saying a few quick hellos, we walk over to the bar to grab a drink. Most of my teammates are already here, some sitting around a booth in the back, others lined up at the bar. Everyone's on cloud nine because although the Sharks aren't our biggest rivals, everyone knows Ford's rivalry with Warner Langley.

Ford's flirting with the bartender when we approach him at the bar.

"Can't you ever just enjoy a guys' night?" Maksim asks him.

"You guys are boring as fuck," is Ford's response.

I flag down the other bartender and order, then look at Maksim. He nods and I order him a vodka. Since this is the Fury hangout after every game, most of the bartenders know us.

"You should be thanking me," Ford says to me, nodding toward the front door.

I turn around and there stands Saige and her friend, Tedi. Why the hell are they here? I'm glad I'll be able to thank Saige in person, but she's in this bar with every one of my teammates who decided to go out and celebrate tonight. There aren't a ton of girls here, which means she's gonna draw the attention of my testosterone filled teammates.

"I figured why should you just be getting it before the game? Celebratory fucks count too." Ford smacks me on the back and walks toward the two women with his arms spread wide, the bartender long forgotten. "Ladies."

Saige looks over and her gaze glues to mine. I shouldn't have the feelings I do racing through my veins. She's my agent's girlfriend—or the woman he's dating at least. I have no idea if they're exclusive or serious, but I'd put money on the answer being no. Not with how much Jaron ignored her on New Year's Eve. Regardless, I need to squash my interest in her and only think of her as a means to an end—she throws the drinks in my face, and I play a great game.

Ford escorts them over to a booth next to some of the other guys on the team and waves me over. I blow out a breath and join them because I'm not about to leave Saige in Ford's hands. Not a chance in hell. The thought of his hands anywhere near her makes me want to choke him.

The waitress reaches them before I do and takes their drink orders. Then I approach the table.

"Shamrock," Tedi says and raises her hand for a high five. "Way to go tonight."

I high-five her back and slide in next to Saige. "Hey," I say like some thirteen-year-old boy who's never talked to a girl. What is my malfunction?

"Hi. Great game."

I want to ask her if she saw any of it because every time I looked at her seat, she was on the phone or not there at all. But that would alert her to the fact I was checking up on her.

"Thanks." I eye her over the rim of my beer, so she gets the point that I'm thanking her for more than the compliment. I'm thanking her for tossing the white wine at me.

Her small smile says she understands.

"So this is what you do when you win?" Tedi looks around the room. "You drink in a bar that has no dance floor?"

"You wanna dance?" Ford asks her.

"Yeah and..." She rises up on her knees and looks around. "Where's Tweetie?"

Ford glances my way and laughs as if this girl can't be serious. I'm sitting right next to her and she's asking for Tweetie?

I snicker as Saige thanks the waitress for bringing her a white wine. I snicker again. Then the waitress sets a bottle of beer down in front of Tedi.

"Tweetie isn't here yet," I say.

"Oh." The disappointment is clear in Tedi's tone. She and Saige share a look that says maybe they should just leave.

I'm not ready to call it a night with her yet.

"You know I'm the right wing, right? Ford Jacobs?" He sticks out his hand and everyone at the table can see Tedi bruised his ego.

"I know who you are." She's obviously not impressed at all. I'm shocked, because usually the ladies love Ford and his flirtatious personality.

"Maybe I need a little good luck charm like Drake." Ford nods in my direction and gives me the once-over.

"Good luck charm?" Saige asks and tilts her head.

"There's no shame in it. You're not the first one to improve a man's game that way."

Damn it. I lower my head.

"Why would there be any shame?" Saige asks, her narrowed gaze on me.

"I just mean that Drake was lucky to find you. You're turning his game around," Ford says.

"Well, he might think it's me, but I don't."

Ford looks at her as if she's insane. "I thought you understood the whole athlete thing. Maksim said you were a social media person or something."

Saige glares at me then leans over the table toward Ford. "What exactly are you under the impression I do for him before a game?"

"Ford." I clear my throat.

He laughs. "I don't wanna embarrass you."

"Embarrass me?" she asks.

I'm desperate to end this conversation and where it's headed. I tug on Saige's sleeve. "Can I talk to you for a moment?"

She doesn't even turn to look at me when she says, "No. Now tell me what Aiden told you." Her voice is more demanding.

"He didn't have to tell me. It was clear." Ford sips his scotch on the rocks and smirks at her. "No judgment."

Tedi grabs his nipple through his shirt and twists. "Tell her what he told you."

"Jesus, woman!" Ford tries to get Tedi's hand off him and looks at me as if I'm actually going to help him. I'd laugh if I wasn't worried about one of them kicking me in the balls.

This whole thing screams immature teenage boy shit, which is not the impression I want to give Saige.

"Get off me." Ford pulls at her fingers.

"Tell her."

"Tedi, it's fine. Let him go. I'm sure Aiden will fess up."

Both women turn toward me, but Tedi has yet to take her fingers off Ford's nipple. I hold my hands in the air.

"Hey, I thought it'd be my nipples getting twisted tonight." Tweetie joins us, sliding in next to me, blocking my escape for after I tell Saige how juvenile I am.

"Tweetie!" Tedi exclaims, releasing Ford.

Ford stares down at his chest and swears again. "Good luck with that one, Tweetie." He slides out of the booth and heads back to the bartender.

Tedi follows him out of the booth, but only to join Tweetie on his side. Damn it all to hell.

Saige scoots farther away from me, but then she's sliding out of the booth. "Take care, Tedi. I'll see you tomorrow at work."

Tedi waves, but she's way more enthralled in Tweetie and his beard.

"Whoa, where are you going?" I follow her.

She stops short of the doors. "Listen, I don't appreciate having rumors spread about me."

"I didn't spread any rumors."

"I'm not an idiot, Aiden. I know what your friend thinks I did for you."

I sigh and run my fingers through my hair. "He assumes because that's what kind of person he is."

"And you didn't correct him? You're just as bad then." She turns toward the door.

I grasp her elbow to stop her. "Wait! I did tell him, he just doesn't believe me. I just… I've never been in this situation before. To need something from someone else to make my game better. It's ludicrous, I know."

Her angry demeanor softens first with her shoulders, then her eyes. "I can't continue on with this if people think I'm sleeping with you just to improve your game."

I hold up my hand. "I know. I know. Give me a minute to clear this up?"

"I should go." She glances toward the door.

"Please? Just give me a second and then let me buy you a drink as a thank you."

She doesn't say anything, so I use the opportunity to embarrass the hell out of myself. I'm going to be razzed about this for years, but it'll be worth it.

I stand on a nearby table, thankful it's a weekday and the bar isn't as crowded as it gets on Fridays and Saturdays. In fact, it's mostly our team here. I use two fingers and whistle to grab everyone's attention. Everyone quiets and I suddenly regret this decision. But I own my mistakes, and for some reason, I want Saige to know that about me.

"Okay, okay! As you all know, I've been out of my funk for the past two games."

A roar of shouts commence.

I glance toward the door where Saige stands. "I've

never been a superstitious guy, as you all know. Never needed it."

They all call out "cocky bastard, arrogant ass, Shamrock."

"But someone has changed that. On New Year's Eve, I met her, and what happened at midnight is what I think has turned my game around."

Saige cocks an eyebrow.

"No kissing and telling!" one of my teammates yells and a few others laugh.

"I didn't kiss her."

"No fucking and telling!" another one yells.

"I didn't fuck her. All she did was throw white wine in my face." I wave Saige over and squat on the table, asking the waitress to grab me a bottle of white wine. "You all need to know that was *all* that happened. That's it. Some of you might share Ford's dirty mind or assume I just wasn't coming out and saying that we slept together but that's not the case. We did not sleep together. And so, I welcome her to do it again as penance for me putting her in the position to be embarrassed in the first place."

Saige shakes her head with a small grin. The waitress comes over and pours the glass, holding it out to Saige. When Saige still refuses, the waitress throws it in my face with a laugh. Then Tedi jumps off Tweetie's lap and pours a glass of wine, tossing it in my face right after with a huge smile on her face. Yeah, she's enjoying this. My tongue slides out and I lick my lips.

"Anyone else?" I ask good-naturedly.

A few of the girlfriends and wives come over and dump more drinks on me with smiles, relishing the opportunity to get in on the action.

I look at the last of the wine bottle and wave it in front of Saige. "Come on. Finish me off."

"Poor choice of words," she says but walks toward me anyway. "You know it was childish to let them think you've had your way with me? That I would even sleep with you in the first place?"

"I do."

She takes the bottle out of my hands and tips it over my head. "I'll forgive you once, especially since you fessed up like a man."

I hop down from the table and the bartender throws me a clean rag to wipe my hair and face. No matter what, this suit is getting dry cleaned.

I look at Saige with complete sincerity because I'm really not one of those guys. "I'm really sorry, Saige. It was never my intent, but regardless, I should've set the record straight as soon as I knew what they thought."

She nods. "Thank you. I appreciate your apology."

"Then you'll let me buy you a drink and you'll stay?"

"Sure."

But as soon as she says it, the door to Carmelo's opens, and Joran steps through. Just my luck.

Saige

$\mathcal{A}$iden and I look toward the door and disappointment washes over me like all that wine just did Aiden. I shouldn't feel let down when Joran walks through, arms raised, shouting to the team about what a great game it was.

He spots Aiden and walks over, but stops short when he sees me. "Saige?"

"Hey, Joran." I wave like an idiot.

Joran and I are far from an exclusive couple. We've gone on one date and a few lunches because his schedule is so busy, so I shouldn't feel as if I just got caught doing something I shouldn't.

He winds his arm around my waist and kisses my cheek. "What a surprise. You were my next call. Just finished up with work stuff."

I smile and let him touch me, but my vision shifts to Aiden, who's intently watching Joran's hand on my hip.

There's no way a guy like Aiden could be jealous of Joran. They couldn't be more opposite. Now that I know him better, I can tell that Joran is the type of guy who's always "on" and I doubt anyone ever sees the real him. Whereas Aiden is quiet and reserved. You never know what he's really thinking, but when he speaks, he means what he says. Those dark eyes are fixed on you, and it's unnerving and electrifying all at once.

Joran dislodges from me and pulls Aiden into that handshake-man-hug thing guys do. "Two games in a row. I told you, you're the man."

Aiden looks at me over Joran's shoulder, and I swear there's guilt lining his face. "Thanks. It feels good to be back."

Joran excuses himself and heads over to the bar. "Give me your best bottle of champagne."

The waitress, who first poured the drink on Aiden and whose name tag reads Brielle, says, "Look around. This isn't the Ritz."

Joran puts his arm around Brielle and whispers something to make her push him off. I catch Aiden glancing at me from the corner of his eye and the entire thing makes me uncomfortable. I feel as though Joran forgot I was even here. Even if we're not exclusive, there's such a thing as being courteous.

"He's just a flirt," Aiden murmurs. "Want to grab a booth? Or go back to Tedi?" The booth where I left Tedi is vacant and Aiden must notice because he laughs. "Man, she works fast."

"It's her fuck-it bucket list," I say as if it's an excuse, but who cares? If she wants to screw Tweetie or whatever his name is, so be it. She's a grown woman and it's her business. "He's a good guy?"

"He'll take care of her," Aiden assures me.

That's all I need to know so that I can sleep well tonight. Not that Tedi can't take care of herself. I've always admired how tough she is.

"Then do you want to sit?" He gestures to a booth.

"Sure."

I lead the way to the same booth we were in before and

slide in. Aiden is polite and sits across from me instead of sliding into the middle of the circular booth.

"Don't you want to shower?" I ask him. He has to be sticky from all that wine.

"Nah. I'm where I want to be."

My face heats with what I'm sure is a blush I hope the dim lighting hides.

"Well, it's not much, but we're celebrating." Joran folds himself into the booth, holding three champagne glasses and a bottle.

"Hey, Brielle," Aiden calls and holds up his beer.

She nods to say she got his order.

"I'm good, Joran, but thanks for the thought," Aiden says. "That shit gives me a headache."

Joran's shoulders deflate, but he recovers quickly, pouring himself and me a glass and raising his in the air. "To whatever the hell got you back on your game."

We clink glasses and Aiden holds his bottle up, gaze on me the entire time.

Ever feel as if you're doing something wrong even though you're not? Right now, I feel as though I made out with Aiden in the back hallway then came out here, but we haven't stepped over any line. Everything between us has been strictly platonic. I owe Joran nothing, but a part of me says that I'm playing games.

"It's me!" I blurt.

Aiden almost spits out the beer he just swallowed, his eyes wide in surprise.

"What?" Joran asks, but his phone rings and he pulls it out at the same time.

"I mean, it might not be me. I don't believe in superstitions and I certainly don't think I'm a part of one."

Aiden purses his lips to stop from laughing as I try to backpedal my way out of this.

To my surprise, Joran silences his phone and sets it on the table. I'm sure I'm not the only one who sees his body tense and his eyes laser in on Aiden. "What exactly did she do to become part of a superstition?"

I throw my hands in the air. "Why does everyone in here think it's sex?"

Is that all these hockey players think of?

"Because they're testosterone-filled athletes," Joran says. "Sex is usually part of the superstition—whether they can have it or not have it, who they can have it with, or whether that matters at all. Ask any player in this room and I bet each one has a superstition about it."

I look at Aiden and he diverts his gaze, sipping his new beer Brielle just dropped off.

"Is that true?" I ask.

Aiden makes a dramatic swallow as if he's taken by surprise. "Joran has a point, but as for me, I've never believed in superstitions, so..." He shrugs.

I swivel around in the booth, looking over the guys and spot who will tell me the truth. "Ford!"

"Wrong person to ask," Aiden mumbles.

Ford comes over and slides in next to Aiden, making Aiden slide closer to me, which means his knee brushes against mine. I ignore the tingles rushing up my leg.

Ford asks, "What's up, sweet thing?"

Aiden eyes him with an annoyed expression.

"Saige," I correct.

"Sorry. What's up, *Saige*?" Ford overemphasizes my name.

"What's your superstition about sex?"

Ford's eyebrows scrunch. "As in how it will affect my game?"

I nod.

"The more the better. I need to have sex in order to

have a great game. One time I had three women at once and I had the best game of my life." He winks at me.

"Told you," Aiden says under his breath.

"So it's normal for athletes to have this superstition?"

Ford looks at Aiden as though he needs his permission to respond. Aiden nods. "Of course. Some only fuck when they win, others refrain during the playoffs, others won't have it with one regular woman, others only do regulars. For some, it can be a specific woman for a specific city we're playing in. It varies."

I shake my head. "Unbelievable." I sip the champagne that's not good at all. I'd much prefer my white wine, but I don't plan to be here much longer.

"Why is it unbelievable?" Aiden asks.

Joran's phone rings again and he excuses himself. Seriously? He doesn't even care to stick around to see exactly what the superstition is? Good thing I'm not invested in what's happening between us.

Aiden's knee touches mine and I suck in a breath before I say, "You guys use women."

"Whoa!" Ford raises his hands. "We're getting used too. Most of those women don't care about us at all. They only want to brag they had us in the sack. Like your friend Tedi." Ford raises a questioning eyebrow.

Aiden says nothing, but I can almost read what he's thinking. Tedi has a fuck-it bucket list.

I concede that point. "Sure, okay, but they can't all be like that. I'm sure you've broken some hearts."

Ford moves his head side to side. "Who's to say my heart hasn't been broken?" He can't even keep a straight face before bursting out laughing. "There are all kinds of hockey players. There are some married men, guys who have steady girlfriends or boyfriends, some like Drake here who finally believes in superstitions and is having his agent's girlfriend throw wine in his face." He shakes his head as though he's disappointed in Aiden.

"I'm not Joran's girlfriend," I clarify, and immediately wish I could take back the words.

Just then, Joran returns to stand at the end of the table. "Hey, I'm sorry. I gotta go. One of my clients is in trouble." Joran leans over the table and kisses my cheek. "You'll get her home safe, Aiden?"

Everyone at the table is silent.

"I'm sure Drake can handle that, right?" Ford claps Aiden on the back, laughing and sliding out of the booth. "Always a fire to put out, right, Joran?" He doesn't wait for Joran to say anything before leaving us.

"I'll get her home," Aiden says, his eyes on his beer, his fingers picking at the label.

"Thanks, man. And way to go. Keep it up until trade deadlines and we'll have tremendous bargaining power at the end of the year."

Then Joran leaves, out the door as though he was never here in the first place.

I push away my champagne. "What is he talking about… trade deadlines?"

"Hey, Brielle," Aiden calls to the waitress. She turns before heading back to the bar. "Can you get Saige a white wine, please?"

"Actually, I'll have a vodka soda with a lime."

Brielle smiles and nods.

"So is that your drink?" Aiden asks.

"Answer my question first."

He stops twirling his beer bottle around. "Trade deadlines are at the end of February. Rumor is if I don't pick up my game, I'll be traded to another team."

"Just because you're in a slump—as you say," I'm quick to add.

He picks up his head and smiles at me as if I'm some innocent little girl who amuses him. "You don't perform, they don't want you. It's as easy as that."

I can tell he's hurt by the possibility.

I reach my hand out but retract it before I touch him. "I'm sorry. That sucks."

"Exactly why I need you to throw a drink in my face before every game." He looks at me with a hopeful expression.

"There's no possible way that's the reason your game turned around. It's ridiculous."

"But it's the only thing out of the ordinary. And… we did it again and it worked."

"Can I think about it?" I ask. "I mean, how would it even work with out-of-town games?"

"I'd be paying a shit-load to get you flights and hotel rooms, and for the rest of this season, you'd get to travel free."

"I couldn't allow you to do that."

"Why? I'm gaining the benefit." He sips his beer as Brielle brings me my drink.

"Thanks," I tell her, and she smiles. "When is your next game?" I ask Aiden, thinking I'll have a few days to consider it.

"Day after next, then I'm on the road for five days."

"Aiden, I have a job."

"A job you can do from anywhere, right?"

I sip my drink and stare at the lime twirling in the ice cubes. It's a hard decision because even though *I* don't believe it, I know he truly does think the drink in the face is helping him perform. Plus, I'm not stupid. I know what'll happen when he doesn't need me anymore. I'll be cast aside like I was with Jeremy. And Maverick for that matter. Even if Aiden and I aren't an item, the way my heart races in Aiden's presence tells me I'll be heartbroken again.

"I think I'm going to get going." I open my purse, but Aiden gets his wallet out first and throws a few twenties on the table.

"Let's go." He stands and puts his hands in his slacks pockets.

It's so unfair that a man can look that good in a suit. So unfair that I can't let myself indulge in said man. "You don't have to take me home."

"Joran asked, and I agreed. Plus, I wasn't about to let you go home by yourself. I mean…" The color in his cheeks deepen and I smile at how shy he comes across sometimes.

"I know what you meant. Thank you."

We walk out of Carmelo's and he pulls out his phone to grab an Uber. "I'd drive, but if I get pulled over smelling like wine, it won't be good."

Ten minutes later, the Uber arrives, and we slide into the back of a sedan. His body is so large, takes up so much space, that I can't help but wonder what it would feel like over mine.

Damn it, I need to remember my mantra about professional athletes. You'd think I would've learned that lesson already.

CHAPTER 7

"I'd rather be the reason you're winning than the
reason you're losing."

Aiden

I've tried to give Saige until the very last second,
but I'm on the way to the game now, and if she
doesn't throw a drink in my face before I take the ice, I'm
screwed.

My phone rings as I drive toward her office with the
hope that she's still there.

"What's up, Maksim?" I ask.

"I just left your girl's office."

"She's not my girl," I say, checking my blind spot
before changing lanes.

"She's not Joran's either. You know that, right?"

"The reason for your call?"

"Did you hear what happened?" he asks, as though he
has a piece of juicy gossip the paparazzi would be eaves-
dropping to overhear.

"What?"

"Maverick Sanders isn't using her anymore."

"I didn't even know he was." I haven't looked into
Saige's business—mostly because I don't care one iota
about social media. I think it's great if she enjoys it, but I
have no reason to see what her business is all about.

"He's her main guy. The one who is pictured everywhere. Spokesperson for her entire company. I guess he was her first client or something."

"And he quit using her?" I frown.

Maksim laughs. "Get a hold of this." He's silent for a second. "This was on his Instagram this morning. It's a picture of Maverick and his fiancée in bed with a tray of fruit and bagels with a caption that says, 'Lazy Friday mornings with my girl.'"

"I don't see the big deal with that." I slow as I approach a red light.

"The problem is you see more of her than him, and having girls on your social media is a no-no. Everyone knows female fans don't want to be reminded that you're living happily ever after with someone else."

"Maybe, but it shouldn't be a big deal. She's a part of his life. His *real* life, not the persona people put on for social media." I'm happy to pass the time talking to Maksim, if only so I don't have to stress about what I'm gonna do if she's no longer at her office.

"They need to think you're unattainable. Come on, Shamrock, use your head."

I guess I see his point.

"Anyway, I just thought maybe you'd want to know since last I checked, you hadn't had a drink thrown in your face yet."

"What, are you keeping tabs on me?"

He laughs. "You're my guy."

"Bullshit." I make a left turn then change lanes.

"Okay, okay, you are my guy, but I wanted to make sure she wasn't mad at you for your Neanderthal move the other night."

"I can make up for my mistakes and idiocy on my own, but thank you." I turn into the parking lot where her office is.

"Well, now you have some leverage."

I think for a moment. Maksim is right. If her biggest client left, she's probably desperate to replace him. Not to be an arrogant ass, but I'd be a good replacement. Then again, I don't want to subject myself to the bullshit on social media.

"Why don't you be her main guy?" I park in a spot and wonder which car is hers.

"Because I'm not Aiden Drake and because I don't need anything from her. You can't expect her to give up her life and follow your schedule for nothing. Come on, use your head."

I do not need this speech from Maksim. "Thanks. I can handle this."

"See you at the arena, and you better have white wine all over that pretty face of yours."

I hang up without saying goodbye and stare at the building. I'm out of my fucking mind to entertain his suggestion. I could go to the game tonight and take my chances that my game will be fine. She's dating Joran and my feelings for her aren't platonic. I'm only asking for trouble. Not that I want to marry her or anything, but I'm definitely not about developing a friendship with her, if you catch my drift.

Yeah, I don't need to jeopardize my career even more by fucking up my relationship with my agent.

I leave the parking lot, driving straight to the Fury stadium. There's no way my career can really rest in the hands of a gorgeous blonde's ability to throw a drink in my face.

*M*y teammates all eye me when I enter the locker room, but I'm not in the mood to be their entertainment. I'm sure they all want to make sure that I got wine thrown in my face today. I take off my jacket, hang it up, and sit on the bench in front of my locker, loosening my tie.

"So?" Maksim sits next to me wearing nothing more than his jockstrap.

"Don't worry about it." I unbutton my dress shirt.

He runs his hand over the front of my shirt. "It's not soaked. I don't like this."

"Maybe I changed." I shrug.

"Maybe you're lying. I don't understand why you'd be so stubborn to not make the deal. I gave you the golden ticket."

"Because it means being on social media again." My mind drifts back to the incident, but I quickly steer my thoughts away. I don't want that on my mind when I step out onto the ice tonight.

His big hand lands on my shoulder and a deep look of sympathy leaks from his blue eyes. "That's in the past. Things are good now, right?"

"Right now, but who knows what could happen if I open all my accounts back up?"

I have no time to even think about it, because Joran busts into the locker room as if he's the head coach. "Gentlemen, have a killer game tonight."

Maksim stands and continues to get dressed, at least covering himself up.

When Joran comes over to me, I ask, "What are you doing in here?"

"I'm here because when I went to pick up Saige for our date, she said she had somewhere else to be." His stance widens and he shoves his hands in his pockets, looking at me. "Then she asked me if I could get her in to see you before the game. Care to explain?"

I stare at him. "Didn't she tell you?"

"She said it's about the superstition thing we started talking about after the last game."

Maksim hums beside me while Ford turns up the volume on his speaker. I stand and tug Joran out into the hallway away from everyone, but I stop short when I find Saige leaning against the opposite wall, looking gorgeous.

She's wearing jeans and a T-shirt with a jacket over it. Her blonde hair is down in waves, and her lip gloss highlights her delectable lips. Fuck me, I swear I just went half chub.

She pulls a small bottle of wine from her purse and dangles it in the air. "Did you forget?"

"I'm starting to feel out of the loop here, guys." Joran pulls me out of our bubble.

"That's the superstition—she throws wine at my face. She did it on New Year's Eve, before I knew you two were…" I don't finish the sentence because I can't for the life of me get myself to say the words. It's hard to admit that I lost out on the one girl who's made me feel something in years.

"Shut up?" Joran laughs dramatically, bending forward and clapping. "You hit on my date?"

A few trainers walk down the hallway, fist-bumping me and staring at the spectacle named Joran.

"That's awesome," Joran says when he finally calms.

I'm glad one of us thinks so.

To Saige, I say, "I didn't think you wanted to do it, so I was going to play without it."

Something crosses Saige's face—maybe regret or

sadness, I'm not sure. I try not to look too hard so Joran isn't tipped off that I'm pining away for his date.

"Well, I still don't believe in it." She shrugs. "But I'll do it."

"I love this." Joran nods at Saige. "Open the bottle and throw it in his face."

"You're in agreement?" I ask him.

I look at Joran and he shrugs. "Why not? I think it's great if it gets your game back."

Saige is quiet a moment. Even though I don't know all her expressions, I'd say right now, she's slightly pissed off. "You think it's great that I might have to travel around with Aiden until this season is over?"

Joran nods. "Why wouldn't I? Whatever gets my number one man back on his game. That's all that matters." He clamps me on the shoulder and beams.

Saige tilts her head. "So you're cool with me spending time with Aiden?"

Joran must finally hear it in her voice and his eyes narrow a bit. "Am I supposed to be jealous?"

"I don't know, I'd think that maybe you'd be a little concerned. He is a professional hockey player and it's not like he's bad to look at."

My ego inflates a little and I will say I don't hate it. Maybe these feelings aren't one-sided.

"Saige, it's not like——" Joran starts.

She shakes her head and cracks open the wine bottle. "Let's just get this over with."

"Joran Peters, get the fuck out of my locker room area!" Coach Vittner yells from down the hall.

"Coach," Joran says with that fake adoration in his voice. He walks over to Coach, leaving Saige and me alone.

She's ready to throw the wine in my face, but I place

my hand on hers and wait for her to look me in the eye. "Thank you. I didn't want to pressure you."

She laughs softly. "I didn't want to be the reason you lost."

"So maybe you do believe in superstitions." I raise an eyebrow.

She chuckles. "I'd rather be the reason you're winning than the reason you're losing."

I swear she's talking in code and there's a lot more underneath that sentence than she's telling me.

I stuff my hands in the pockets of my slacks. "Do your worst."

She laughs and throws the wine bottle toward my face. Not nearly the normal amount of wine comes out, so she continues to do it until the small bottle is empty.

"Let's hope the cheap stuff works just as well as the expensive stuff," I say while I wipe my eyes.

She looks at the bottle. "This is the most expensive they had. Good luck tonight. I'm going on record as saying you didn't need me to do this."

I lean forward, my hands still in my slacks, my tongue sliding out to lick the sweetness dripping from my face. "Then why are you here?"

Our eyes lock and neither of us looks away. For a moment, it's just us in that hallway.

"Drake, get your ass in the locker room!" Coach screams. "Joran, take your girlfriend and go back to the suite. I feel like I'm back coaching at the college level." He disappears into the locker room.

Joran laughs and points at me. "Looks like it's all handled?"

I nod. "Thanks, Saige," I say, hoping she hears my sincerity.

"Have a great game," she says with a smile.

Joran holds out his fist to me. "Knock 'em on their asses."

We fist-bump, then Joran slides his hand into Saige's. I watch them walk down the hallway while my chest constricts painfully. I head back into the locker room to find Maksim already getting his change of guards from Tyler outside the bathroom. He raises his hand to high-five me, seeing that my shirt is now soaked.

"Another time." I decline since he's just come out of the bathroom. Who knows what other superstitions he has?

I quickly get my gear on, thinking about how I can't help but like Saige even more now that she sought me out to make sure she could dump the drink on me. It says a whole lot about her and the fact I can trust her with my social media. So tomorrow, I'll open myself up to the piranhas of fandom once more. Hopefully I don't land in court again.

Saige

The office is dead silent because Tedi is running late. Her personality fills the space when she's here.

I'm sitting at my desk, stewing after last night. The Fury won their game and Aiden scored two goals. At one point, I swear he looked at me in the suite, but it could have been my imagination. It *has* to be my imagination. Although on New Year's I felt that pull toward him, felt that he had some interest, I'm sure it was only to get in my pants. Now he just needs me to throw a drink in his face.

There's a knock on the door, and since I'm the only one here, I walk over and peek through the side glass. Aiden stands there with a folder in his hand, wearing low-slung jeans and a T-shirt with an open hoodie. His hair is styled to a messy perfection, and those dark eyes are smiling at me. God, he looks like he could be in a high-end jeans ad. It makes it hard not to stare.

I open the door and welcome him in. "Is there a game today?"

I walk back to my desk, fully aware I'm giving him a view of my ass that's snug in my pants because of the amount of junk food I've been consuming from stress eating over his proposal.

"No. I go on the road in three days, so I wanted to sit down and discuss some things with you."

I slide out my chair and sit down, motioning with my hand for him to do the same across from me.

"No Tedi today?" he asks.

"She's running late."

"Another fuck-it bucket list item scratched off last night?" He smirks at me, and I can't help but smile back.

"She's a rare breed, but she's also the best friend a girl could have."

"I figured that out when she titty-twisted Ford's nipple."

We share a laugh. What would I do without Tedi?

"Great game last night," I say to break the tension.

"Thanks. I guess the drink throwing did the trick again. How was the suite?"

"Well, all the food and drinks you can consume and the people below looking up at you with envy." I shrug. "But honestly, I'd much rather be in the stands. Everyone up in the suite is just schmoozing and hardly watching what's happening on the ice except when a goal is scored." It's not like I'm a die-hard hockey fan but if I'm there, I want to watch the game.

"I figured. I'd rather be with the fans too. I feed off of their energy."

I don't mention that I noticed that when Tedi and I sat in the first row. Aiden and some of his teammates actually communicate with fans. Either to read their signs, or give a puck to a little kid, or razz another player. It's endearing and makes them less like idols and more like everyday people.

"They love you."

"As long as I keep scoring they will." There's something more under those words, but he clears his throat before I'm willing to ask. "Anyway, I'm here with a proposition for you."

I lean back in my chair. "Another proposition?"

"I know that if you come on the road with me, it'll only inconvenience you." He looks around the office. "You have your business, and it was insensitive of me to suggest you could drop everything just to tag along with me."

Huh, this is interesting. "Joran seems to think I should do just that."

"Joran would sell his firstborn to make sure my game is on point." I open my mouth, but Aiden raises his hand. "I'm sorry. I shouldn't have said that."

"It's fine." I got that impression when Joran was more than willing to let me throw wine at his client in order to make sure he got what he needed.

"Not really, but that's between you two." Aiden meets my gaze then glances away.

"Yeah, it is."

There's no way I can tell Aiden I'm not really into Joran. I wasn't even going to go on our date yesterday, but I knew I had to get behind the scenes and Joran could get me in. After he pushed me at Aiden, he's not really someone I want to be involved with. I want to be some-one's number one and not so easily cast aside or pushed away. But I have the sense that if I break things off with Joran, Aiden might try a little harder to win me. With my shaky willpower, I'd eventually end up on his back porch like every other puck bunny in history.

"Anyway, let's go through this," he says. "As you may or may not know, I own social media accounts in my name, but I do nothing with them. Signing up was a way for me to make sure people knew any accounts posting as me were fake. I hate everything to do with social media, but Maksim said you lost Maverick Sanders as a client?"

I want to bury my head in my hands right now. "Let me just stop you right there. You do not need to be his replacement."

"Then you'll travel with me to all my games through the rest of the year for nothing?"

When he puts it that way, he does have a point. He must see something cross my face because he smiles and nods as though he's right.

He passes the folder across the desk. "These are my usernames and passwords. The only thing I ask is that you keep my family out of it. Don't friend any of them and don't mention any of them."

I accept the folder and open it, seeing a list of his family's accounts at the bottom. In big bold letters, it says DO NOT CONTACT OR FRIEND. This is obviously serious to him.

My forehead creases and I look up at him. "You don't have to do this if you're not comfortable."

He sits back and rests his ankle on his knee. "You're helping me, I'm helping you. I'll pay you whatever Maverick was, and if you want me to be your spokesperson, done." He nods toward the brochure on the corner of my desk, Maverick's face plastered all over it.

I blow out a breath and think about what this means—the kind of involvement we'll have in each other's life if I agree to this. But how can I say no when I do need someone big like Aiden Drake on my client list now that Maverick is off?

"I don't know what to say." Truly, I don't. It feels as though this is huge for him. Going from no social media to handing it over to someone he barely knows takes a lot of trust.

"Just say I've got a better mug than Maverick." He winks and stands. "I'm kidding. There's nothing to say."

When he's standing, he feels so tall. I can only imagine what it's like when he has his skates on. He's probably like a tree. That thought makes me want to climb him.

"Turn the page and you'll find your itinerary of planes, hotels, and tickets to all the games. I included two in case you want to bring Tedi with you so the two of you can work. My practice schedule is listed in there. Other than that, I'm at your disposal. All I ask is that you're there early for each game so I don't have to chase you down."

I suck in a deep breath then let it out. "Okay."

He nods, a small amount of fear lacing through his dark eyes. "Thanks for doing this, Saige. I know it might seem crazy, but I'm desperate to keep this streak going."

"You're welcome, and I'll try to make the social media stuff as painless as I can."

He laughs and steps back. "There's nothing painless about social media, but I trust you. See you in Philly."

Then he turns and walks toward the door. I admire his ass until Tedi barrels through the door and Aiden steps back, only to have her spill her coffee all over him.

"Fuck," he says, backing up and pulling the shirt off his skin. "That's hot."

Tedi looks him over. "I agree."

Aiden tears off his sweatshirt, then grips the collar of his T-shirt and pulls it over his head, leaving him bare-chested in the middle of my office. Holy shit, the man is cut. And he has tattoos from his shoulders to his elbows.

"Is this the new dress code? Because I'm game." Tedi puts down her cup and pretends like she's going to undress.

"Tedi," I say, standing and rounding my desk.

The closer I get to him, the closer I am to licking his chest. Screw chocolate sauce, caffeine-filled abs like his is my new wet dream.

"I'm sorry," Tedi says, but her eyes can't stop focusing

on the way his jeans are hung low, showing us the treasure trail leading to a place I'm pretty sure neither of us would object to seeing.

"It's okay." He waves out the T-shirt, but it's no use. He tucks it in the back pocket of his jeans, puts his sweatshirt back on, and zips it up.

I'm not sure if it's Tedi, or me who makes a whining noise now that he's covered up again.

"Are you sure? I can wash it," Tedi offers. "Along with my panties now."

Aiden rolls his eyes and smirks at Tedi. "Don't tell me you want to work your way through the Fury lineup. Is that on your fuck-it bucket list?"

She gives him an annoyed look and shakes her head in teenage girl fashion. "Tweetie is enough to handle."

"That's just because you haven't had me." He winks and laughs good-naturedly.

I hate that his occasional arrogance turns me on. But what I hate even more is him flirting with Tedi.

"Okay, Tedi, let Aiden leave."

Tedi leans forward. "She's just jealous because she's got Joran. He probably answers phone calls mid-orgasm."

I stare at her blankly as she laughs with Aiden. Although she could be right, I have no idea because I have no interest in sleeping with Joran.

"Bye." I wave to Aiden.

"Thanks again. See you soon." Aiden walks out of the office.

Once the door is shut behind him, my head falls forward. I envision what I could actually do with a man like that if he was mine. Or even better, what a man like that would do to me.

"Jealousy looks good on you." Tedi points at me and drops her coffee in the trash can.

"Why would I be jealous?"

"You got all flushed when I flirted with Aiden."

"I don't know what you're talking about." I might as well bite the bullet with Tedi now. "And by the way, we'll be traveling a little bit."

"For what?" she asks.

"Because Aiden Drake is our new spokesperson. In exchange, I have to throw white wine on him before every game."

Her perfectly arched eyebrows rise. "You're serious?"

"I am." I nod.

"Then can we make a wager?"

"No."

"Come on. I bet you sleep with the man before this is all over."

I shake my head. "I can't sleep with him. He's a client now."

She shakes her head. "One day you'll realize rules are meant to be broken, Saige. Especially when he's got a body like that."

I wish I could say I disagree with her.

Aiden

I arrive in Philly with the team and head straight to the room I'll be sharing with Maksim. The plane ride wasn't too bad since we ended up playing the Oh Hell card game, which is the whole reason Ford is ignoring us—even though we're on the same floor and our rooms are right next to one another's.

"Rematch, Jacobs?" Maksim eggs Ford on as we head down the hall, towing our suitcases. We all end up outside our rooms, key cards in hand.

Ford waves his card in front of his door and it buzzes. He enters, leaving Tweetie shaking his head at us.

"Thanks a lot, assholes," Tweetie says. "Now I'm stuck with a pissed-off roommate."

"He'll get over it," I say, and we enter our room after Tweetie flips us off.

Once we're in our room, I take off my jacket and hang it in the closet before sitting on the edge of the bed to take off my shoes. Maksim, on the other hand, flops face-first on the mattress.

"You're gonna get wrinkled," I tell him even though he doesn't care. He never does.

He rolls over. "So how are we playing this? The old sock thing?"

I take off my other shoe and lie back on the bed, exhausted after being up all night debating if I made the right decision with Saige. It's hard to trust that people will do what they say when you're in the public eye. But if she's helping me, it's only right I do the same, especially since she didn't ask for anything to begin with.

"What are you talking about?" I ask.

"Your girl is in the hotel. It's cool if you want to get it on. Just let me know. I would be pissed if someone saw my girl naked."

"Do you have a girl I don't know about?"

"Hell. No. But if I did, no one would see one inch of her skin."

"So what? When you find the girl you want to marry, she's gonna have to wear a sheet over her everywhere she goes?"

He sits up on the bed and toes out of his shoes. They drop to the floor one by one with a thud. "No, I'm just not cool with people seeing what's mine."

"Lucky girl," I say with a roll of my eyes.

"You're dodging."

"I'm not dodging. First of all, she's not my girl. Second of all, all I need from her is to throw a drink at me. End of story."

He shrugs out of his jacket and tosses it on the chair across the room. Maksim and I are close in age. We've been roommates when we travel since we started with the Fury and he's my boy, but he's also the biggest slob I've ever met.

"You're delusional when it comes to her."

I glance at him, my forearms resting on my thighs. "She's dating Joran."

"Since when does Joran date? I swear he parties with us just to get into women's pants."

Maksim has a point, but who am I to say which girl can reform a playboy? One day I'm sure there'll even be a woman who will win Ford over. Saige is awesome. She'd be a game-changer for a lot of guys.

"He's my agent and he's done a lot for me."

Maksim unbuttons his shirt. "Let me get this straight. Joran is wherever he is. You're here. Saige is here. You're going to be the go-to guy to keep her company. She's traveling with us to every city, staying in the same hotel as us, just to throw a drink in your face."

I nod.

He stands from the bed, his shirt joining his suit jacket haphazardly thrown on the chair. He claps me on the shoulder. "Good luck, man."

"What does that mean?"

He stops before entering the bathroom. "You don't have the willpower to resist her."

The bathroom door shuts, and I sit there for a moment, thinking his words through. Of course the jackass has a point.

Luckily my phone interrupts my spiraling thoughts. Not lucky—it's the woman in question.

Saige: *We're here. Room 320. Let me know when you need me.*

I pretend I'm not thinking dirty thoughts over her choice of phrase. But I have some time to kill before the game and I'd rather spend it with her than listening to Maksim snore. I'm too wired to rest.

Me: *Want to go tour Philly?*

The three dots appear and disappear, then reappear.

Saige: *Sure. I'll meet you in the lobby in 10?*

Me: *Perfect.*

Maksim comes out of the bathroom wearing only his boxer briefs, throwing the rest of his clothes on the chair.

"I'm heading out," I say.

"Great." He slides under the covers on the bed and grabs the remote. "I'm gonna watch some porn and take a nap before the game."

I'm thankful he doesn't ask me where I'm going and who I'll be with. Then again, he knows I usually go out in the cities we travel to. Why would I stay holed up in the hotel when my job allows me to travel the country? Nothing worse than spending time in a city and only seeing the airport, the hotel, and the arena.

I quickly change into jeans and a sweater, grabbing my winter coat since Philly is fucking freezing. My skull hat might keep me from being recognized, so I put it on, and I grab my sunglasses before I'm out the door.

---

*S*aige is already downstairs in the lobby, looking over the brochure area for tourists. She's bundled up in a jacket, scarf, hat, mittens, and boots. She looks adorable and I wish I was the lucky bastard who could peel away those layers until she was naked in front of me.

I lean forward and whisper in her ear, "Hey."

She jumps. "You scared me."

"Which would be the point." I tug one of the braids on either side of her face. "Cute."

"Well, plane hair sucks and I figure I'll spray them black and white for team spirit tonight."

"You trying to get on the Jumbotron?" I mindlessly pick up a brochure about a science museum.

"Never."

"Oh, come on. The Kiss Cam?"

She knocks her shoulder into mine. "What on earth about me would make you think I'd enjoy kissing someone on camera in front of thousands of people?"

"Some girls dream of that." I put the brochure back. "Shall we?" I wave my arm for her to follow.

"Well, not this one. Tedi handles that for both of us."

I laugh as we circle through the rotating doors onto the streets of Philly. It's just as cold as when I exited the bus a half hour ago. I stuff my hands in my coat pockets.

"What's up, Wisconsin boy? Too cold for you?" She smiles at me.

"I'm perfectly fine. Remember I skate on ice for a living."

She grins. "Touché."

"You're the one dressed like a blizzard is coming."

"I have thin blood. Leave me alone."

I put up my hands. "Noted."

"So where do you want to go?" she asks.

I shrug.

"Would you mind if we go see the Love sculpture? I know it's cheesy."

"Sure. Do you know—"

She pulls out a brochure and I can't help but smile. She's fucking adorable.

"Then lead the way," I say.

We head to the sculpture, our arms brushing one another's but no other contact besides that. Once we reach it, we wait in line. I'm prepared to snap a picture of her, but the man behind us pushes me to go stand with Saige.

"I'll take the picture. Give me your phones." He nudges me forward.

Saige stops mid-stride and looks back at me. I'm sure she doesn't want me in her picture, but what choice do we have at this point? I don't want to make a spectacle of myself and be recognized. That would only ruin my afternoon with Saige.

We stand under the sculpture that spells LOVE in big red letters. It feels natural to put my arm around her back, my hand molding to her hip.

"Take your sunglasses off," the man says.

His wife next to him nods. "You'll ruin the picture!"

Great, I didn't realize we were models. Saige giggles and we plaster on smiles, waiting for someone to take the picture. Finally the couple snaps the picture and we step away to take our phones back.

"Would you like us to take one of you two?" I ask the older couple.

They accept, and after all is said and done, Saige and I are about to walk away.

A man with his family calls, "You suck."

Saige stops walking. "Is he talking to you?"

I nod and usher her away with my hand on the small of her back. "I assume so."

"You suck, Drake. You're gonna be eating ice shavings tonight."

I put my hand in the air to acknowledge that I heard him and continue walking. Saige circles out of my hold to head back toward the man. I turn and grab her elbow nicely, redirecting her the way we were going.

"What? You're going to let your girlfriend fight your battles? Just like you have Petrov do all your dirty work on the ice?"

I'm not surprised to come in contact with a die-hard

fan. I'm in their city. I am a little surprised he's doing it in front of his kids, but who am I to give parenting advice?

"Why don't you have some respect?" Saige yells.

I chuckle, pulling her back. "He's not worth it," I whisper.

She pulls her arm out of my grip. I glance around and see that we're causing a crowd to form.

"Hey, I really wanted to go to the art museum and run up the stairs like Rocky." I try to distract her, but she's not letting me.

"Aiden's a damn good hockey player and he's going to mop the floor with Philly tonight."

I can't help but laugh at the fact Saige is sticking up for me. Half of me wants to throw her over my shoulder, and the other half wants to see what else she's going to say.

"You might be sleeping with him, but trust me, our team is better." The man steps up.

His wife sends me an apologetic look.

"We'll see about that," Saige snarls.

Her comebacks could use some work, but the point is she's going to battle for my reputation.

"He's really not worth it." I tug on her arm.

She rolls her eyes. "You're right. I wish he could go one-on-one with you, then we'd see what he has to say." Thankfully, she turns around to join me walking in the other direction.

The man mumbles something, but his wife tells him the kids are there.

Next, we head to the art museum so I can see the stairs Rocky Balboa ran up. At the bottom, we look at one another.

"Want to race?" I ask.

"Um… no."

I knock her shoulder. "Come on. It'll be fun."

"Maybe for a fully conditioned professional athlete." She points at me. "But not for a once-a-month kickboxer." She points at herself.

"Kickboxer, huh?"

"Did you catch the once-a-month part?"

I tug on her jacket. "It'll be fun, come on."

"You're not going to let this go, are you?"

"Nope."

She situates her purse so it's crossways over her body. "Fine."

"One... two... go!" I yell.

We both rush up the stairs. Luckily we're not the only people reenacting the famous movie scene. Two boys are on the other side of us.

Halfway up, Saige stops and bends over to catch her breath.

I jog in place. "Come on."

"I'm not training to box anyone. Let me alone." She waves at me.

I throw her over my shoulder because, hell... I want to. She squeals and I run up the steps to the top. I shout and throw up one fist.

"Put me down now?" She pats my back, laughing the whole time.

I lower her to the ground, disappointed because I enjoyed touching her, even if it wasn't sexual in nature.

"It's beautiful here," she says, staring across the city.

"Yeah, it is."

"Excuse me, Mr. Drake?" A small voice interrupts us.

I look down to see the kid whose dad just screamed at me. Obviously they're hitting all the nearby tourist stops too.

I squat. "Hey, what do you need?"

He hands me a piece of paper and a pen. "Could you sign this? I've never met a real hockey player before."

Saige sighs behind me.

"Sure. What's your name?" I scribble down my signature and wish him luck.

He stares at the paper with wide eyes and a huge smile. "Thank you."

"Anytime."

The kid leans forward. "Sorry about my dad."

I wave him off. "No worries. You have to stay faithful to your team. Always."

The kid walks back to his mother, and I catch sight of his dad at the bottom of the stairs with their daughter.

"That was so sweet." To my surprise, Saige initiates contact by sliding her arm through mine and resting her head on my upper arm. "After his dad was such a jerk and everything."

I nod, but it's not the kid's fault his dad's a jerk.

"You made his day," she says.

I want to tell her that she made my day. That spending these couple hours with her makes me crave more time with her. But that's not in the cards because she's seeing someone else. Someone who directly affects my own success.

Saige

"*A* photo shoot?" Aiden groans.

"More like a few poses of you in your casual clothes, maybe in your house or something. Just so people can get a feel of who you are off the ice." I slide my chair side to side.

"Just you in bed," Tedi adds. "No worries, we'll cover the important parts with a sheet." She laughs.

He glances at her and sips his coffee. After the trip to Philly, I'd be lying if I said I don't feel more connected to Aiden. The way he handled the obnoxious fan, the way he picked me up, the fact that he's not at all like what anyone would picture a professional hockey player to be.

"I can put on my Speedo and we could go to the beach," he jokes.

"Perfect." I smile. "Just make sure they're the super low ones so we can see those hip indentations."

He moves his hands to cover his chest and crotch. "I feel dirty now."

Tedi laughs from her desk.

"The other thing is… would you mind if I follow you around for a day?" I bite my lip because I hate asking this. I'm sure he'll hate the idea. "We could invite Maksim and kill two birds with one stone."

He holds up his hands. "Hey now, I don't kill innocent animals."

I tilt my head. "Har har."

He shrugs. "Sure. Actually, Maksim and I are going fishing tomorrow morning. Want to join us?"

I scrunch up my eyebrows. "Fishing? Don't people wake-up really early?"

"Not much of a morning person, huh?" He sips his coffee.

"No, but I'll make do. I'll bring my camera and do some candid shots of you both. Tedi?"

"Hell to the no."

Aiden turns around in his chair. "What if I told you Tweetie was coming?"

Tedi blushes. I'm as amazed by her reaction as Aiden seems to be. While we were in Philly, she was never in our room. From what I heard, she and Tweetie rented their own room because Ford said he wasn't leaving his and Tweetie's.

"I'm curious, did that fuck-it bucket list include 'have a relationship with a hockey player' on it?" Aiden asks.

Tedi balls up a piece of paper and throws it at him. "I never thought it would happen, okay? But I'm not through with him."

Aiden turns to me and raises his eyebrows.

I lean over and whisper, "Is he really a good guy?"

Aiden scrunches his eyebrows at me and finishes his coffee before throwing the cup into the trash can.

"I'm going to the bathroom," Tedi says and walks out of the office, leaving Aiden and me alone together.

"So is Tweetie a good guy?" I ask again.

Aiden stares at me. "What kind of answer do you want? The one I should give the best friend of the girl he's banging or the truthful one?"

I stare at him. "Seriously? That bad?"

"Nah." He waves me off, dropping his foot so both are on the floor. "He's a good guy. If Tedi wants something serious, he might too." He shrugs. "I mean, he's not a perpetual bachelor like Ford or anything."

"Hmm… she rarely puts herself out there. I mean, she's been with him more than once."

"Is that like Guinness Book of Tedi's Records or something?"

"Kind of. Ever since I've known her, she's never wanted a boyfriend or any kind of commitment." I shake my head. "And I probably shouldn't be having this conversation with you. So back to fishing."

He laughs. "It's cool, I'm down with the girl talk."

I open my drawer and pull out some paperwork. "I'm sending these home with you for you to fill out. You can give them to me tomorrow. Let me know if you have any questions."

He groans. "You're giving me homework?"

"I do travel all over creation for you." My eyebrows rise, and he chuckles.

"Technically, you've traveled once. Which reminds me, when we head to New York, my cousin is having an adoption party. Her husband is adopting her daughter. I thought maybe you'd want to go with me?"

My eyes widen and my heart trips over itself. Is he asking me out on a date?

"Completely platonic, of course. I'm getting them tickets to the game that night and they'll be sitting with you, so I thought you might like to meet them beforehand. Their daughter, Jolie, is the best thing ever. She's seven and loves me because hello, I'm the best hockey player ever." He raises his shoulders as though he's bragging.

"Oh, well, um… sure." I'm unsure how to answer. It's

weird that he's asking so early. What if the drink thing is already off the table by then because it stops working?

"I have to give her a head count, and I figured this way you're not stuck in the hotel room the whole time either."

I laugh. "You did say New York City, right? I'm pretty sure I could find a thing or two to do."

His smile falters. "Oh, then by all means, you don't have to come with me."

There's something weird in his expression, like he's disappointed I might not go.

"I'm happy to go. You're right. It would be nice to meet them before we're all watching the game together."

His cloudy expression clears. "Great. I'll let her know. She's been on my ass about it."

"Perfect."

We sit in silence for a moment before he stands. "How's Joran? I haven't heard from him in a while."

Funny he says that, because I haven't either. "He's good."

"Good." He knocks on the corner of my desk. "All right. See you tomorrow."

"Can you text me the address?"

"Definitely."

He walks out of the office and I lean back in my chair, unsure what exactly is happening between us. Then I head to the window and wait the three minutes it takes him to ride the elevator down and head out to his SUV in the parking lot. He walks out of the building threading his fingers through his dark hair, then circles his keys around his finger. When he stops at the driver's door, he glances toward my office. I'm thankful for the mirrored windows so he can't see me. Then he slides in and drives away.

"What are we looking at?" Tedi whispers in my ear and I jump.

She and Aiden clearly have the same sense of humor. "Nothing."

"Bullshit. You were checking him out." She sits on the edge of my desk. "Let's get real for a moment, shall we?"

I walk over to our small kitchen area where there's a coffeemaker and a few snacks. "Let's drop it. He's a client."

She turns to look at me. "You can tell me."

I can trust Tedi with anything, I know that. But admitting anything to her is admitting it to myself too. I can feel myself almost bursting though, dying to talk to someone.

"He's an attractive guy," I say. "A really nice guy. By all accounts, a decent guy. Of course I'm kinda into him, but I don't date athletes anymore."

"Oh please. Aiden and Jeremy are on two opposite sides of the field."

"You say that now, but their lifestyle is very similar—on the road, girls galore, anything they want at their fingertips." I refill my coffee mug and head back to my desk.

"Not everyone will take advantage of that." Tedi has her serious look going. The one that suggests I need to forget Jeremy and move on.

"Okay, okay, enough personal talk. Time to get to work." I shoo her off my desk.

She hops down and heads over to hers.

"Also, if you keep asking me questions about Aiden, I'm going to ask you about Tweetie. What is his real name anyway?"

She laughs. "I haven't a clue."

I shake my head. Maybe that inkling in my stomach was wrong. Maybe Tedi doesn't see anything more than sex with Tweetie.

*T*he next morning, I'm in jeans and a sweater with a jacket over top. My hair is flung into a messy ponytail and my makeup isn't the best it could be. Who gets up at this ungodly hour to catch fish when you could buy them in the grocery store?

I head down to the marina. Surprisingly, I see a lot of people loading different boats with fishing poles and coolers.

"There's the beauty of Aiden's eye!" Maksim yells from what looks to be one of the biggest boats in the marina.

Even the other boaters groan, because it's still too damn early for that.

"I have no idea what you're talking about. And we need to discuss your comment on Twitter last night." I point at Maksim and accept the hand he's offering to help me into the boat.

"What? That guy thought he'd school me on vodka? What the fuck ever. Then he told me I'm a sellout because I play here in the US? What am I supposed to do? Just let that shit go?"

I drop my bags on a bench. "Yes. That's exactly what you're supposed to do. I'm your social media person now. At least call me to consult before you go off on someone publicly."

He shrugs. "I don't want that fan anyway."

"It's not about wanting the fan, it's about keeping your cool. Who the hell cares about vodka brands?"

"Oh, you did it this time. He might just throw you overboard." Aiden comes up from under the deck, and the sunrise does wonders on a face. While I look as if I just woke up after a bender, he looks refreshed and gorgeous with the backdrop of yellow and orange sky. "Good morning."

Aiden winks and I melt, almost losing my footing and falling to the bench.

"Good morning," I choke out, hopefully sounding unfazed.

"I told you that whole vodka thing was bad." Aiden slaps Maksim on the shoulder and comes over to me. "Do you get seasick or anything?" He offers a pill in his hand.

"No, I should be okay."

"Perfect." He pockets it and his gaze roams up and down me. "Amazes me how prepared you always are."

"I wouldn't say I'm prepared. This is extremely early, and I've never fished in my life."

He grabs ahold of my hip and slides by me. "Then I can't wait to be your teacher," he whispers in my ear, causing a flutter of goose bumps to race up my spine.

He goes behind the wheel and starts the boat.

"Is this boat yours?" I ask.

Aiden nods rather than talk over the sound of the engine starting. Maksim must be on the boat a lot because they work together like pros to get away from the dock. Then Maksim sits in the front of the boat, watching it move through the water. I decide to take a few candid pictures of them. A far away one of Maksim at the front of the boat, and one of Aiden driving.

"What's her name?" I ask, raising my voice over the engine noise and the wind whipping past us.

"*Twilight.*"

"I didn't peg you for a fan."

He looks at me with a crinkled forehead as though he doesn't understand.

"Team Jacob or Edward?"

His head rolls back between his shoulder blades. "I named her *Twilight* because I love taking her out right as the sun sets."

My mind plays tricks on me, thinking about being here with him. Us anchored in some secluded area while I'm stretched out naked for him. "Sounds like fun."

He laughs, his gaze on me as though he knows what I was thinking. "Maybe another time we can leave Maksim home?"

I stare at his lips. So full and pink. I wonder briefly what they would feel like on mine. How does Aiden kiss? Hard or soft? I clear my throat. I shouldn't think like that.

"Did you finish your homework?" I ask, changing the subject.

"My dog ate it," he says, but nods toward the downstairs part of the boat. "Just kidding. It's down there. We'll be anchoring in about twenty if you want to go down and have a look at it. Or wait and enjoy the wind in your hair."

"It needs to be about twenty degrees warmer for that," I say with a wry smile.

He reaches toward my ponytail. "Do you mind?"

I hesitate for a second and then shake my head. He expertly undoes my ponytail and my blonde hair fans out, blowing straight back behind me.

I close my eyes and relish the breeze flowing through my strands even if I do have a slight chill. "Oh, that feels good."

When I open my eyes back up, Aiden's staring at me with a smoldering expression that has me thinking maybe I don't care so much about consequences anymore.

Aiden

*M*y phone rings while I'm in the lobby of our Denver hotel, waiting for Saige to come down. Luckily, this hotel is used to having sports teams, so other than one guy stopping and asking me if I'm Aiden Drake, I've been left alone.

Joran's name flashes on the screen. I've been dodging him as much as I can lately because I'm heavy into his girl and that's not cool, even if I have no plans to do anything about it. Since I'm about to see him because I'm shooting a commercial and Saige is coming with to grab some social media shots, I might as well get it over with. All three of us will be thrown together soon enough and I'll have to endure the sight of them together.

"Hey, Joran," I answer.

"How's my favorite center? Plane ride good? Who won your card game? Tell me you beat Ford."

I nod and laugh because Ford can't win Oh Hell to save his life and it's becoming more comical the longer his losing streak continues. "I'm good, and Maksim won this time."

"Did Ford have a shit fit?" He chuckles.

"How'd you guess?"

"Sorest loser I know. Thank god he's not my client, what with his anger issues."

He makes Ford sound like a bad guy. At least Ford pays for all the damage he does.

"I'm just waiting on Saige, then we'll head over to the studio."

"Perfect. I'm almost there too. Had a meeting first."

To be honest, I have no idea what Joran does the majority of the time. He's got all different clients, but when I was in my slump, he was up my ass nonstop and now he's nowhere to be found. I'm not even sure why he's babysitting me with this commercial campaign.

"Okay, we'll see you there," I say and hang up as Saige makes her appearance.

"Do you ever go anywhere warm?" she says.

We both look outside at what I think might be a blizzard starting.

"At least the sun's out." I point toward our view of the mountains.

We walk out of the hotel and the doorman flags a taxi to take us to the shoot location, which is a bit out of the city. I'm happy to have more time alone with Saige, even as fleeting as it will be.

"Did Tedi come?"

"Tweetie's here, isn't he?" She chuckles. "I ran into Tweetie coming out of the elevator on our floor when I was leaving. I'm not so sure about those two."

She files into the taxi and I tip the doorman before sliding in right next to her.

"Pretty soon you'll be a bridesmaid."

She balks. "Tedi? Marriage? Never."

"Why's that?"

She shrugs. "You heard her. She has a fuck-it bucket

list. Who has one of those and is looking for a serious relationship?"

She's got a point. "You do know if I had a fuck-it bucket list, you'd think a lot less of me."

She looks at me with my favorite smile of hers on her plump lips. The one that says I'm right but she'll never admit it. "Maybe. Like if your buddy Ford said he had a list of women he wanted to sleep with—"

"I said myself. Why are you switching it to Ford?"

She laughs. "Because you're not like that."

I stretch my arm out along the back of the cab bench and give her my full attention. "How do you know that?"

Her eyes lock with mine for a second and her smile dims. "I guess I don't."

I lean across. "I'm kidding. You do know me. I'm not that type of guy."

She doesn't say anything and shifts to watch the world go by while we make our way to where the shoot is happening. The silence isn't uncomfortable per se, but I get the impression she had something more she wanted to say to me but didn't.

The taxi eventually stops, and I hand some money to the driver through the window then step out. I want her to know I'm not that guy, but more importantly, I want her to know for certain in her gut that that's not me. I'm not out picking up women after games. Something in my own gut tells me she's been hurt before, even if she's never expressed as much.

I hold my hand out for her, helping her out of the taxi.

"Thank you," she says.

We walk into the arena where the commercial is being shot and find Joran waiting for us. It's one of the rare times he's not on the phone. He smiles and heads over, shaking my hand before hugging Saige and kissing her cheek.

"Aiden Drake." A woman comes out, her hand already poised for a handshake midway toward me. "I'm Gia Santos, and I'm your bitch today."

I laugh and shake her hand. "I promise not to take advantage."

Gia's eyes sparkle. She's attractive. Dark hair, dark eyes, and an exotic look I'm sure helps her with the guys. She points at me.

"He's trouble, huh?" She poises her question to Saige, who looks momentarily put off by what she just witnessed, but she snaps on a fake smile quickly enough. I've been around Saige enough to know when her smile is genuine or not and this one isn't.

"This is my agent, Joran Peters, and—"

"My girlfriend, Saige," Joran interrupts, and my gaze falls to the floor.

Saige gives him an annoyed look, then returns her attention to Gia. "I'm also Aiden's social media advisor. I hope it won't be a problem if I create a little buzz about the commercial by taking some pictures?"

"I'll talk to my boss, but as long as you don't give away any details—since it's a new product launch—I think we're in good shape."

"Perfect." Saige smiles more genuinely this time.

The two women walk in front of me, and Gia talks as she escorts us to one of the locker rooms. "There will be two wardrobe changes today. First, we'll have you on the ice with some kids. Second shoot will be in the locker room."

I nod, understanding the drill. This isn't my first shoot. I just hope I can concentrate with Saige here.

"We should probably let you get ready." Saige hovers by the door with Gia.

"Yeah, I'll kick it here with him if you're cool with that, Saige," Joran says.

Gia turns to Saige. "Hungry?"

"Sure." She shrugs.

The women leave, and I turn to Joran. "You don't need to stay with me."

Joran sits on the bench across from me. "No biggie. I've barely seen you since your game's back. Speaking of…"

I grab the outfit they want me to wear on the ice and undress. When you've spent almost your entire life in a locker room full of naked guys, you tend not to be too averse to nudity.

"Have you seen the psychologist yet?" Joran asks.

I shake my head. "No."

"Well, Gerhardt was pretty firm on that. I'm sure he's happy you're playing well, but make that appointment pronto. You still have to be an altar boy until trade deadline."

I shrug off my slacks and put on the track pants and team jersey they brought for me to wear. I eye the skates but decide to leave them until right before I get on the ice. There's a makeup chair set up at the far end, so I head over there and take a seat. The next part of this will be them putting fucking eyeliner on me.

"He should be happy I'm scoring goals. Period."

Joran leans forward. "I talked to him last week. He's ecstatic, but you know how these things go. Once a player gets in a slump, that's all people remember for a while. I'm just suggesting that you keep up everything he wants you to do. And keep Saige at your disposal to throw a drink in your face before every game." He laughs and doesn't notice that I don't join in.

I clench my fists from hearing him say she's at my

disposal as though she's a beach house I can stay at when he's not using it.

"What's up with you two anyway? Girlfriend?" My attempt to bring it up casually doesn't come off as flippant as I would like, but if Joran senses anything, he doesn't acknowledge it.

"What was I supposed to say? This is the woman I hook up with?"

I pull out my phone to distract myself and hope he can't see right through me. "So that's all she is… a hookup?"

He laughs. "What's with the big brother act? I get that the two of you hang out now, but you know where I stand on relationships."

I thought I did until I wanted the girl he saw first. "I've never heard you call someone girlfriend before, that's all."

"It was easier than to explain. Plus, what does that Gia care anyway?"

A knock sounds on the door and I'm thankful for the reprieve so I can compose myself and quell my incessant need to drill him with questions about Saige. It's the makeup team, and I welcome them in.

Joran stands. "I'm heading out to meet up with Saige. See you out there, big guy."

The makeup artist compliments me on my dark eyes and how mysterious they are. I don't have to sit in the chair too long before Gia comes in and grabs me for the shoot. I pick up the skates they've supplied and head out to the ice with her. There's no sign of Saige or Joran anywhere.

"You think you can beat us tonight?" Gia asks with a smile.

"Are you a hockey fan?"

She shrugs. "I don't follow extensively, but I can't say I

mind watching hot alpha men skating on ice and letting their tempers flare."

I chuckle and nod. It's not the first time I've heard that, and it probably won't be the last. "Glad we can entertain you."

She says nothing and brings me over to meet the director and the kids who will be in the shoot with me. They're decked out in their hockey gear and head out onto the ice.

"So from what I'm told, I'm just teaching them how to play?" I ask the director.

He nods. "You got it."

I sit down and tie my skates, looking up every time I think I hear someone coming, but it's never Saige or Joran. I sigh. This is a problem. I figure I should get this commercial over with and go back to the hotel. Maybe I should pick up a girl tonight to channel these feelings that are consuming me. At this rate, Saige is gonna become a distraction, not a source to help my game.

I skate out to where the three kids are and fist-bump them all. I push the puck around with my stick and one kid tries to steal it and I laugh, following him. Instinctually, I give him some instructions on his footwork. The other two kids come over and I show them a drill to work on their back skating.

I swear it's not more than twenty minutes when the director calls cut. I feel like we barely even got started.

"Whoa, you're awesome," Gia says when I get off the ice. "Really good with kids. Got any?"

I laugh. "No."

The director has me do two more scenes with me skating through the rink and stopping quickly to hold up the sports drink. Then one more where all the kids are around a table with a pizza, drinking the same drink. I fist-bump the kids, tell them they did a good job, and head back to my locker room. There's still no sign of Saige or Joran.

Gia opens up my locker room for me. "Change into the bag marked 'wardrobe number two.' There's a robe in there to wear out if you prefer. I'll be back in five."

I open the bag and find a pair of boxer briefs and a robe for the locker room scene. Since I'm by myself, I take off what I'm wearing and use a Sharpie to sign the jersey, leaving it across the back of the chair.

I'm pulling on the boxer briefs when the door springs open. I turn to find Saige there and freeze. Her gaze roams down my body until it lands on my dick. She fixates there enough that it twitches as if to say if she keeps looking, I'm gonna be hard in five seconds flat.

"Saige?" I say.

Her eyes flick to mine. Her cheeks flush as though I just said the dirtiest words to her, which makes my dick think it's definitely time for him to show himself in his full glory. I hurry and slide the boxer briefs all the way up before I embarrass myself further.

"I'm sorry." She turns and slams the door.

I stand there trying to calm myself so I don't go out to shoot the rest of this commercial with a fucking hard-on.

CHAPTER 12

"I'm not naïve enough to think it's the
first one you've ever seen."

Saige

I strip my arm out of Joran's after he leads me into some supply closet. "What are you doing?"

"I thought we could have some fun while Aiden's filming the commercial." He leans toward me, and I put my hand on his chest.

"Did you miss the part where I have to snap some candid pictures for his social media?" I step back, but his hands land on my waist, tugging me closer to him.

"Do you really? Who cares? All the women want is to see him half naked." He bends over to get to my neck, and I shove him off me. His back hits a metal rack and a bottle tumbles off the shelf to the floor.

"How about you try taking my profession seriously?"

He laughs and holds up his hands. "I do. I do."

"Then why would you think I was here to make out with you in some disgusting closet rather than take pictures for Aiden?"

He looks at me long and hard. "What's up with you two?"

I can't help but get an uneasy feeling, so I shift my weight from one foot to the other. "Exactly what do you think?"

"Do you like him?" His eyes narrow the slightest amount.

"No." I should've been crossing my fingers, but even if I did like him, there is no chance for Aiden and me. There's no way I'd put myself in that position again.

"Come on. He's a big shot hockey player, flying you all over, putting you up in hotels. I see his social media accounts… I assume it's you he's exploring cities with."

I cross my arms. "Do I like him as a person? Yeah, he's really nice. And oh yeah, he calls me more than you ever do. Speaking of… why are you here right now, Joran?"

"Because it's a shoot that I arranged for him. A sponsorship."

I roll my eyes. "Do you go to all your shoots with your clients?"

"The ones where the girl I'm seeing is there, yes." He crosses his arms now.

"So a few dates, a few phone calls and texts, and now we're dating?"

He steps toward me. "What would you call it?"

"I'd say that you asked me to your boss's house on New Year's Eve, followed up with a few lunches and a hockey game, and now you think I'm screwing your client, so here you are to make sure I'm not." I jut out my hip.

"You're wrong."

I shake my head, ready for this to be over anyway. "Regardless, we should probably end this. Whatever this is. I'm too busy to be at your beck and call. Plus, I want a guy who would've picked me up at the hotel today to bring me here."

"Why, when you could come with Drake? I wasn't anywhere near the hotel."

I huff and stare at him. "One day, some woman is going to twist your world up and you're not going to know what to do about it, but I'm not that woman. So." I pat his suit-ladened chest. "Have a great life."

I open the storage closet and walk out, sucking in a deep breath. I feel as if a fifty-pound weight has been lifted off me as I walk down the hall to the ice rink. I end up off to the side and I snap a few pictures from far away as Aiden's having pizza and drinks with the kids. He's adorable the way he ruffles their hair and laughs at whatever they're saying.

Gia comes by and says it's time to go, but he takes the time to sign things for each of the kids before heading back to the locker room to change.

I feel good about dropping Joran. He's not a bad guy, but he's definitely not relationship material. The end of us was inevitable anyway.

Before heading to the locker room, I stop at the refreshment area and take a cookie, needing some sugar in my veins before I have to confront and deal with whatever this is developing between Aiden and me. We can't do anything about these underlying feelings. I know men like Aiden, and he's a prime candidate to hurt me. What is it that they say? Fool me once, shame on you, fool me twice, shame on me? I learned my lesson with Jeremy, and I'm not a fan of repeating my mistakes.

I grab a Diet Coke and head back to the locker room. I'm hoping Joran doesn't return to set anytime soon. If not, things will be awkward.

Maybe I'm too wrapped up in my mind with what just happened with Joran, but I open the door to Aiden's locker room without knocking and all I see are naked body parts flashing before my eyes. Legs, thighs, hands, arms, stomach… oh shit, is that? I blink. And stare. Yep, it is. I'm staring directly at Aiden Drake's dick and I'm not diverting my gaze. It's like I can't control my eyes.

They.

Will.

Not.

Move.

I haven't been with a ton of guys, but this might be the most beautiful dick I've ever seen, which is probably because it's attached to the most gorgeous guy I've ever seen. Of course he'd have a perfect cock and of course I'd get a good look at it, so I know exactly what I'm missing.

The clearing of a throat finally jolts me from my stupor, and I balk. "I'm sorry."

I rush out and shut the door. Gia bounces down the hall toward me.

"Joran wanted me to tell you and Aiden that he had to step out." She smiles brightly. "How's our guy doing?"

Should I say hung like a horse? Probably not. Where is Tedi when I need her?

I clear my throat. "He should be out soon. You know, I might just run out to…" I step forward to head… anywhere but here. Maybe hop in a cab and go back to the hotel.

Gia clasps my elbow. "You barely got any pictures with the kids. Plus, I'm sure all the ladies will love seeing his abs on display."

I smile tightly and the locker room door opens.

"Perfect. You're ready to go. Come on." Gia starts off down the hall.

I peek over and Aiden's standing there in a white terrycloth robe. Let me tell you, I've never been a robe person, for myself or anyone else. But damn, he makes something a mom of four would wear after a long day sexy as hell.

"Gia, can you give me a minute with Saige?" Aiden asks.

My heart drops to the depths of my stomach. Can't we just act like nothing happened?

She stops and turns around. "Sure. We're down the hall to the right. Not too long though." She smiles and continues on her way.

I step away from Aiden until my back hits the wall and I close my eyes, hoping this will be quick so we can carry on like it never happened. I feel his breath on my face before he speaks.

"Open your eyes, Saige," he whispers, and shivers run up my neck.

I peek one eye open and he chuckles.

"We're adults," he says. "So you saw mine. I'm not gonna ask you to show me yours."

I open my eyes. He's being so adult about this and I'm acting like a thirteen-year-old girl. "Well, I know that. I wasn't worried about you wanting to see mine."

He places his finger to my lips and steps closer, his body pressed right up to mine. My nipples pebble in my bra. "I wasn't finished."

"Oh."

"Unless you want to show me yours." He winks and laughs as though it's a joke. Does he think this game is fun? Because I'm hanging on by a frayed thread here. "Honestly though, it doesn't have to be a big deal. Just forget it."

"Okay." I'll never forget that vision for the rest of my life, but I can pretend to. He may have just ruined every man's opportunity with me in the future.

"Let's go get this over with." He motions for me to walk down the hall, so I do. "Where did you disappear to before?"

"Oh, Joran needed something. He had to head out, by the way." I say it casually with the hope that he won't ask me any more questions. I'm going to keep quiet about the fact that I broke off whatever I had with Joran because it acts as a barrier between Aiden and me. And after what I just saw, I'm gonna need all the fortification between us that I can get.

"So just us two heading back to the hotel?" he asks.

"I guess so."

"Good. I have somewhere I want to take you first."

I open my mouth to say no, but Gia ushers us into the room with a set made to look like a professional locker room. It even has Aiden's last name on one of the lockers.

The director heads over to us. "So, we've decided to change it up. We're going to put you in a towel and get you wet so it appears you just got out of the shower. Then you'll head to your locker, sit down, look at the camera, and say, 'After a win, I only drink…'"

Crap. I'm stuck here because I have to take pictures, but I really should excuse myself. The last thing I need on top of everything else is visions of Aiden taking a shower swimming through my head.

"And, Saige, we haven't forgotten about you. Can you take some pictures and short videos as we're prepping him? We think that'll be good for social media and get people anticipating when the commercial will come out." Gia smiles brightly, but I want to scream and run away.

"Great," I choke out.

Aiden laughs. "Saige, you ready to get me all wet? You're always so good at it."

I narrow my eyes. He thinks this is funny? "Remember Tedi with Ford in the booth at Carmelo's?" I remind him of the titty-twister. "You might be next."

I watch as he hikes up his boxer briefs so they won't be seen in the shot. At least they're not being perfectionists and actually having him be naked.

Gia thrusts a water bottle in my hands. "Can you spray him down?"

I make the mistake of looking at Aiden, who smirks as if he's loving this entire situation.

"Payback is a bitch," I remind him.

"Hey, I'll spray you down anytime you want. Just ask."

I shake my head. "You're incorrigible."

"And you love it."

God help me, but he speaks only the truth. I spritz water on his chest, and it makes his skin glisten like a juicy apple. Man, do I want to take a bite.

"All over, Saige," Gia says.

Why exactly can't she do this?

Aiden spreads out his arms.

I spray it on his shoulders, down his abs, and his stomach retracts a bit. "Is it cold?"

"A little."

"Worried about shrinkage?" I grin.

"Not with you around."

"Aiden!" I whisper-shout.

"Relax, I'm just having fun with you."

Little does he know his fun is making my lady parts clench so hard I could crack a walnut down there.

After I spray him all over—even his stunning face with those damn pouty lips that are now pink and inviting—I back up and take a picture with the spray bottle in the foreground. Then I do a video of my hand spritzing him. He's so photogenic he probably could've been a model if hockey wasn't his thing.

"All right, let's get started," the director says.

I sit in a chair off to the side, and it only takes Aiden five takes before he's done. We both say thank you to everyone, then we're walking down the hallway toward the locker room.

"I'll wait outside," I say once we reach the door.

"You don't have to be shy. It's only a dick. I'm not naïve enough to think it's the first one you've ever seen." He opens the door and holds it there.

"Of course not. Not that I've seen a ton. I mean, I'm not a virgin, but at the same time, I don't…" His laughing spurs me to stop speaking. I point at him. "Just go change and I'll wait out here for you."

"Gotcha." He shuts the door and my back falls to the wall in defeat.

He doesn't yet, but if we keep up this flirting, he just might have me, and that poses a big problem, at least for me.

CHAPTER 13

"You always did love the athletes."

Aiden

I take Saige to my favorite juice bar in Denver. She seems impressed I'd actually go to one and can decipher the menu.

"Want to walk for a while?" I ask.

"You never want to be in the hotel room, huh?" She sips her drink, opting for something with a lot of fruit.

"I get bored, and when I sit around all day, I always have a shitty game." I turn us toward a park so that I have less of a chance of being recognized.

"That makes sense. I should snap a candid of you enjoying your juice before the game." She takes out her phone. "Pose?"

"Do you want duck lips?"

She laughs and snaps the picture of me with duck lips, my juice straw sticking out of the side of my mouth.

"Why don't we take one together?" I suggest.

She shuts down the phone and puts it in her purse. "Nope."

"Why not?"

"I'm still building your fan base and most of them right now are women. Women who want to date you."

"And?" I take another sip of my juice.

"And you're not a dumb jock, Aiden, you know exactly

why." She sips her juice and continues walking, looking up at the bare trees.

"Why don't you enlighten me?"

She gives me an expression that says, "Come on, you don't need me to explain it to you." But explain she does. "Women don't want to see you with another woman."

"But you're just a friend," I say—to be truthful, it's just to see her reaction.

She looks at me quizzically. "You consider me a friend?"

I put my arm around her shoulders. "Of course. Do you not consider me a friend?"

She rolls her eyes and weaves out of my hold. "I thought I was your bitch." She smiles at me and finishes off her juice, tossing the cup in a nearby trash can.

I chuckle. "Oh, you're not my bitch. And you are my friend whether I'm yours or not."

"Don't act like I've offended you."

I slow my footsteps, finishing my juice and tossing it in the trash too. "You did a little. There aren't a lot of people I put in that category."

"Well, don't I feel like an asshole now. Why would you put me in that category?"

I glance over from the corner of my eye to not make it obvious how much she intrigues me. How much I enjoy sharing something like this—a walk in the park—with her and how it's something I'd enjoy doing every day. But she's involved with someone—my agent—so I can't lay my cards out like that.

"When you brought that bottle of wine down to the Fury arena and used Joran to get to the locker room to see me, you moved into the friend zone. You didn't have to do that, but you did."

"We made a deal," she says simply.

I shake my head. "Not at that point. I'd stopped at your office on my way down to the game, prepared to ask you to throw the drink in my face, but I didn't go in."

"You did?" Her forehead wrinkles.

I nod. "I thought I shouldn't put any more pressure on you. I mean, what do you owe me?"

She swivels around to walk backward so she can look at me. "Can I ask you a question?"

"Depends," I say warily.

"How hard is it being a professional athlete? I mean, I think everyone on the outside sees only the perks. Since I handle the social media for a lot of athletes, I see the flip side at times, but even I think it has to all be worth it." She turns back around and walks at my side.

"Ever since I can remember, this is where I wanted to be. In the national league, skating. Not for the money, although yeah, it's nice. But because I couldn't imagine doing anything else. But the road to get here was hard and full of ups and downs, and there are never any guarantees. You lose track of friends and teammates because of trades. Maksim and Ford are probably my best friends, but if I get traded to another team, it's like starting all over again. Eventually we're just saying a quick hello before a game or catching up afterward. And the guys with families have it worse. When they get traded, they have to upend their entire families. Their kids leave their schools and their friends. It's rough for everyone."

She winds her arm through mine and rests her cheek on my shoulder as though it's a natural thing we do all the time. "Surely you have friends who aren't professional hockey players?"

"Friends who are *ex*-hockey players. Since most of my time growing up was spent playing, most of my friends existed in that world too. The majority of them didn't make it to the professional level and are married now. When I go home, I visit and stuff, but it's not like they can understand what my day-to-day life is like. All they see are the perks, like you do." When she doesn't respond right away, I say, "First world problems, I know. But they're problems just the same."

It wasn't my intention to have this "woe is me" conversation with Saige, but she doesn't think what she did for me that night was a big deal. It absolutely was, because she expected nothing in return.

"I have a confession," she says, removing herself from my side. I inwardly groan when she's not next to me anymore.

"Do I want to know?"

"You're nothing like I imagined. That night at the party, I thought you were just some cocky guy hitting on me even though you knew I was there with someone else. But right now, you seem like the polar opposite of that guy."

I nod. "I'm still a 'see what I want, take it' kind of guy. That doesn't go away. It's how I got into the NHL. Not accepting the word no. Never giving up hope. But I hope you feel like I've respected your situation with Joran since I found out."

She looks at me and tilts her head down. "You do flirt."

"True, and if you want me to stop, I will. Just say the word. But know that I'm not doing it to cause problems between you and Joran. It just seems like the default way we communicate."

She's quiet. I think she's gonna ask me to stop and I'll never see that pink flush to her cheeks again, but she never says anything. It would never be my intention to try to steal Joran's girl, but what is he thinking, leaving her with me so much? There's no way he can't see how she's not the type of girl who comes around twice in a lifetime. Surely Saige wants someone more attentive, and even if that guy can't be me, I hate seeing some guy treat her badly—even if it is my agent.

"Oh my god!" Saige screeches and grabs my arm, pulling me down onto a nearby bench.

It's cold as fuck and my ass rejects the metal, but I ease back down when Saige hovers her face in front of mine so that the back of her head is facing the path. I hear laughter from a couple walking by us, and Saige's breath is fast and labored. She closes her eyes when the guy talks, and when she opens them again, her expression pleads with me not to say anything. As if I would. The only better position would be her straddling me and her lips actually on mine.

Once the couple has passed, she pulls back. "Thank you," she mumbles.

"No problem. Care to explain?" I stretch out on the bench, putting my arm behind her.

She stares in the direction the couple went. "That was my ex, Jeremy."

My head swivels to try to catch sight of the bastard who let her slip through his fingers, but the path curves around some shrubbery and all I catch is their laughter. "Does he live here in Denver?"

She shrugs. "I don't really know. After we broke up, I promised I'd never look up anything about him and I've adhered to that."

"Hmm." I frown at the look of discontent on Saige's face.

She nods. "Yeah, let's go." She tugs at my jacket and stands.

I rise off the bench, but the same laughter from before rings closer. Saige's eyes widen.

"Want to throw me on the bench again? Maybe this time we could actually make out?"

She playfully pushes me, grabs my hand, and tugs me down the path.

"Saige?" a deep voice filled with curiosity says from behind us.

She stops and stares straight ahead, unblinking for a moment, drawing in a deep breath. She doesn't even have to ask; I lower my hand and entwine our fingers.

Circling back around, I'm not prepared for the man standing there to be almost as big as me. Hell, he might have a few more muscles than me. The girl at his side looks similar to Saige except she's a strawberry-blonde. Nevertheless, they look like a happy couple.

"Jeremy?" Saige says with faux surprise.

We all move closer to each other, and holy shit, I do a double take. Her ex-boyfriend is Jeremy Danders? The wide receiver for the Packers?

"Whoa, talk about crazy." He steps away from the girl and wraps Saige in a hug. "It's been so long. You still in Waterfall Springs?"

"Yeah." Saige backs up as soon as is polite.

"I heard you've made a success out of that social media thing."

She nods.

I clear my throat, and not waiting for Saige, I stick out my hand. "Aiden Drake."

"The hockey player?" he asks.

I nod. "We're playing Colorado tonight. Saige comes with me to a lot of the away games."

"Really? I thought you NHL players shared rooms."

"We do. I put Saige up in her own." I link our hands again.

Jeremy's gaze shifts to Saige. She doesn't say anything

but squeezes my hand, presumably in thanks. This is the least I could do for her.

The girl says his name in a sweet tone, and he shakes his head. "Oh, sorry, this is Olivia."

"His fiancée," Olivia adds, taking off her left glove and raising her hand. There sits a sizable engagement ring.

A strangled sound comes from Saige. I try my best to save her, but I'm thinking Jeremy might not only be an ex, but *the* ex who broke her.

"Congratulations," I say. "So are you still playing for the Packers?"

I don't follow football religiously, mostly because our seasons overlap and I'm too focused on my own to watch football.

"Rumor is I might be traded here. We decided to make a weekend of it to see if we like the area. Hence how we're lost in a park somewhere." He looks at Olivia and they both laugh.

Shit, they're the real deal. Saige's hand goes limp in mine at witnessing their interaction.

"That sucks," I say.

"Not really, we'd rather be here with the mountains than in Green Bay," Olivia chimes in.

"Except that the fans love me up there. More than in Florida, that is." He sets his gaze on Saige and I wonder what the story is there. "Hey, I know this is crazy, but why don't we all get together for dinner tonight?"

"Can't," Saige is quick to say. "Aiden has a game."

"Game?" Olivia asks.

"I—"

"He plays for the Florida Fury. Hockey," Saige says before I can respond.

"You always did love the athletes." I don't think Jeremy meant it as a slam, but it kind of comes off as one.

Saige looks away. "We should go. Aiden needs to get ready for the game and everything. Nice seeing you, and congratulations."

I'm about to say congratulations when she twists me around and we walk in a direction I'm not familiar with.

"Wait!" Jeremy calls. "How about a nightcap? We're always up late anyway. It'd be nice to catch up."

What is this guy's problem? He's clearly moved on, so why doesn't he leave it alone?

"Um…" Saige looks at me.

I kind of like this fake boyfriend role I've found myself in, so I make a snap decision. "Sure. How about I leave some tickets for you guys at will call, then after the game, we'll be at a bar called Giggling Grizzly."

"Oh, you know how tired you get after a game," Saige says like a concerned girlfriend.

I shrug. "One drink won't kill me."

She sighs and narrows her eyes a bit at me. I kinda love it when she's a little angry with me. It makes me think of how awesome our sex could be.

"Perfect. We'll see you then," Jeremy agrees, and we all walk away from one another.

As soon as we turn a corner and are out of sight, Saige smacks my arm. "Why would you do that?"

"It'll be fun. Trust me. But I do expect to hear the story about you and Jeremy at some point."

She groans. "A *friend* wouldn't put me in this position."

I put my arm around her. "Sure they would, because this is going to close that door on Jeremy for good. And something tells me that's what you need."

CHAPTER 14

"I lied earlier."

Saige

Sitting in the stands of the arena, I throw my head back in annoyance once again that Aiden agreed to drinks with Jeremy and his fiancée tonight. Of course this is the first trip that Tedi hasn't joined me. Not to mention I think the two empty seats to my right are for the happy couple, which pisses me off even more because Aiden got them the seats. It's one thing when he'll be next to me, but another when he's on the ice.

Plus, I usually try to distract myself at his games because he looks hot as hell skating around, yelling for the puck, scoring like the god he is. I don't want to have to watch any more of the game than I absolutely have to since he's already the one I'm thinking of when I touch myself every night.

The teams take the ice for warmups and Aiden steps out, not wearing his helmet, so his sexy face is there for all to admire. And they do. Even though we're in Colorado, there's a pretty big fan section for the Fury full of signs with Aiden's number, women screaming for Ford, and guys rooting for Maksim.

As they skate by me, each player gives me a wink. Poor Tweetie looks a little lost without Tedi. Hopefully that doesn't hurt his game.

"Man, these are great seats." Jeremy folds himself in next to me.

I slide as close as I can to the guy on my other side. Jeremy practically has the entire concession stand in his arms. Olivia, sipping a soda, sits down next to him.

"There's something kind of mean about hockey. Don't they fight?" Olivia asks.

"Hell yeah, it's the best part. Tell Aiden thanks for the seats." Jeremy looks at me with a genuine smile.

Did I just enter the Twilight Zone? Because when we broke up, I swore I'd never see him again. Yeah, it's been a few years, but I still harbor ill feelings toward him. How can he not know that? Does he not have any unresolved issues from our breakup? Of course, why would he? He's the one who broke up with me after moving me across the country.

"Sure," I say.

A stick hits the partition and scares me so much I almost jump out of my seat. Aiden's standing on the other side of the glass. Still no helmet.

"There's Aiden," Olivia says.

Smart one he's got there.

"Thanks, these are awesome!" Jeremy yells, pointing at the seat.

Aiden nods and smiles at them. Tonight was the first night I really enjoyed throwing the drink in his face, what with this stunt he pulled.

He crooks his finger at me, and I stand as he mouths "sorry" and points toward the Jumbotron. I narrow my eyes, not understanding what he's talking about. Then I see a video on the screen of me throwing a drink in Aiden's face. We did it in front of Maksim tonight and the bastard recorded it.

"All hockey players have superstitions," it says at the

bottom of the screen. "Anyone as curious as us to know how this one started?"

I stare blankly at Aiden. Maksim comes to a stop next to him, laughing his ass off. I shake my head at Maksim, but he pats Aiden on the back to get going. I fall back into my seat and cover my face from embarrassment.

"You gotta tell us what that's about," Jeremy says.

"No, I don't." Jeremy is the last person I'd tell that I'm only here with Aiden due to his superstition and that we're not really a couple. I glance at Olivia and mentally compare myself to her. How come he proposed to her and not me? What makes her so damn special? "I'm going to get a beer, do you guys want anything?"

They both decline and I walk up the stairs, really wanting to continue walking right out of the arena. After getting a beer, I hover at the top of the stairs, not ready to go back down to my seat. I watch Aiden take the face-off and he wins, passing the puck to Ford, who skates down the boards. Ford shoots it to Aiden, who's coming down center ice and passes the puck to Tweetie, who flings it to Aiden just before circling the back of the net. Aiden backhands it and scores.

I smile as he raises his hands, falls to his knees, and slides for a second—his signature move after winning a goal. After everyone hits him on the head in congratulations, he looks at my empty seat. His smile dims and the look on his face tugs on my heart. I wonder for the millionth time what we're doing.

The friendship thing surprised me on our walk, but he's right. Somewhere in all of this, he has become my friend. As weird as that is. And friends support friends.

I walk down the stairs, sit next to Jeremy again, and decide that tonight I'm cheering Aiden on.

For the next three periods, I'm screaming, yelling, and

banging on the glass. Even Aiden's eyebrows are raised when he skates by, but he always rewards me with a wink. One time he even blows me a kiss. He's really taking this fake relationship thing far.

When the final buzzer rings, Fury has won, two to one.

"Man, that was an exciting game. Nonstop action." Jeremy shakes his head.

Olivia spent the majority of the time on her phone, but Jeremy was actually cheering with me at one point.

We stand, and I'm stretching when Aiden skates over to the glass. "I'll meet you there in thirty or so," I can just make out over the sound of the crowd exiting the building.

I nod. Great, now I have to go by myself to the bar with my ex and his new fiancée. Perfect.

***

There's a booth open, so I beeline toward it right as we get in. It's in the back, which will help with people not coming up to Aiden. Of course, Jeremy gets stopped a few times on our way through. I forgot about him.

"I love it here," Olivia gushes as the two of us reach the table.

Once we're seated on opposite sides of the booth, I ask, "Where did you two meet?"

"We met in Milwaukee. I was out for a bachelorette party, and he and a few of the other players were at the same club. We chatted a bit. He called the next day and now." She holds up her hand. "We're engaged."

I fake a smile, but there must be something about it that she can tell isn't completely genuine.

"I know about you, you know," she says. "And I think it's absolutely horrible what he did to you."

I'm surprised Jeremy shared that information with her since it doesn't exactly cast him in a positive light. "Thank you, but it's been three years now. I'm good."

"Oh, great." She looks over her shoulder where Jeremy is still talking to a group of guys. "He felt absolutely awful about it, even when we met. He said you two just didn't have the stuff to make it long term."

I swallow the bitter comeback that's clawing up my throat. "Should we order some drinks?"

I smile and raise my hand for a passing waitress, and she tells me she'll be right back.

Jeremy finally joins us, sliding in beside Olivia. It's weird seeing him do the same moves with her as he once did with me. He rests his arm behind the bench, and she slides in close to him. They do make a cute couple, and they'll probably make good-looking kids.

"Did you guys order anything?" he asks.

"The waitress hasn't come over yet," I say.

Jeremy grabs the waitress's attention and of course she heads right over, and we all order our drinks. She returns with menus, and I absentmindedly let my gaze drift over it. If I told Tedi to guess where I am right now, she'd be as likely to guess correctly as I am to slide down a unicorn's rainbow tail someday.

The half hour with the three of us is excruciating, but when Aiden walks in, I forget the entire uncomfortable night. His hair is still slightly damp from the shower and he's dressed in his suit. Tall, dark, and handsome aren't strong enough adjectives to describe him.

He searches the room, mindlessly saying hello and shaking hands with a few fans. When our eyes meet across the bar, a wickedly delicious smile crosses his face, as though he's been waiting all day for this opportunity. I can't deny that it feels great to have that expression poised in my direction.

Winding through the crowd, Aiden reaches us and slides in next to me. Instead of wrapping his arm around me, he places his hand on my thigh and kisses me just under the ear. I whimper and close my eyes briefly.

"Great game," I say.

"Thanks," he whispers in my ear.

"Yeah, man, when you took that hit in the second period, I thought for sure you were out," Jeremy says.

He pats his side. "I'm little banged up, but luckily we have four days off. I'll heal."

"Is it bad?" I ask, concerned.

"You can kiss it later and make it feel better."

I smile and roll my eyes playfully at the act he's putting on.

The waitress comes over. I'm not surprised she's willing to stop for Aiden like she was Jeremy. "Can I get you anything?"

"Just a water please."

"Water?" I shift to face him a bit.

Aiden looks at me. "I took some pain pills for my side." Then he turns back to the waitress. "But I will have eight buffalo wings, chips and queso, and a bratwurst. You getting anything?"

I shake my head. "No, I'm full from the game."

"You can snag some chips and queso off my plate like usual."

"Thanks."

Jeez, he plays the part of doting boyfriend well. It's like he's done this before.

The waitress looks at Jeremy, and he says they're good but asks for some refills on their drinks.

"Bratwurst, huh?" Jeremy says. "No one makes them like they do in Wisconsin."

"I know. I'm from there originally."

Jeremy shuts up then.

"So Saige throws a drink in your face before every game?" Olivia asks.

Aiden glances over and squeezes my thigh even though they can't see it across the booth. His hand has moved up an inch since he got here. Not that I'm paying attention.

"It's how we met," he says. "She thought she could resist me, but turns out I have too much charm."

"Sure, that's it." I laugh.

"Come on. You couldn't resist me that first night." He nudges me with his shoulder.

"You'll never know," I singsong.

"One day I will." He locks eyes with me, and I swallow because sometimes I forget how breathtakingly beautiful he is.

"You guys are really in love," Olivia says, resting her chin on her hand and looking at us dreamily. "The chemistry is wafting off you two. If everyone could have what you guys have."

"And what we have." Jeremey tugs her closer to his side.

"That goes without saying." She gives him a peck on his cheek, but Jeremy is staring at me.

Finally the food arrives and Aiden scarfs it all down except for the few chips and queso I sneak off his plate. Aiden pays the entire bill with his credit card, and we file out of the bar before it gets too late.

We stand on the sidewalk a little awkwardly for a minute before I say, "Bye, guys. I wish you both luck."

I put my hand out and Olivia shakes it, but when I do the same to Jeremy, he pulls me into a hug.

"You look really good, Saige. Happy."

"I am," I respond, lying because this whole thing has been an act, but he doesn't need to know that. It's apparent from spending time with Jeremy at the game that he doesn't follow hockey. He won't be looking for me at all of Aiden's games for years to come.

After Aiden wishes them well, I watch them walk down the street hand in hand. It takes me a minute before I hear Aiden telling me there's a cab waiting. I slide in and still can't tear my eyes away. Seeing Jeremy with someone else only makes me question myself, because at one time, I thought we were destined to be together.

I'm not sure if my face shows it or not, but Aiden puts his arm around my shoulder and pulls me into his side. I lay my head there and welcome the comfort of a friend.

Looking up at him, I rest my hand on his chest. "I lied earlier."

"About what?"

"You are my friend."

The brightest smile I've seen from him transforms his face, and I go back to resting my head on his shoulder and let my eyes drift closed. Even if we can never be more than friends, this feels good too.

Aiden

*A*fter a reprieve in Florida, we're on a flight headed to New York City. It's three weeks until trade deadlines and my game has never been better. I've scored and assisted in every game since Saige started throwing wine on me. This time, since I'm heading into town early to spend some time with my cousin, Frankie, and her daughter, I get to fly with Saige.

We've just stepped onto the plane and she situates herself in first class, pulling out a book and buckling her seat belt. She looks so organized and poised, I want to go all animalistic on her and dirty her up. If only she were mine.

Joran's been MIA lately, saying he's got a problem client and as long as things are cool with me, he'll be in touch after the trade deadline to make arrangements for a new contract at the end of the season. The selfish side of me has no issue with him keeping his distance because I've been able to see Saige more than ever lately.

She insists on posting more social media content since we're still in the *building phase*, as she calls it. I only go along with it because it lets me go places like the zoo with her.

Today I want to get her on the ice. I rented a rink for a

couple hours. She doesn't know it yet, but I'm teaching her how to skate this afternoon.

"I would have been happy in coach," she says, accepting the glass of mimosa from the flight attendant.

I shake my head. "But first class is better."

She smiles. "You've been spoiling me."

As the plane taxis away from the gate, the flight attendant comes by and takes our mimosas. Saige gets comfortable with her book and I check out the cover. It's some self-help book.

"What's that about?" I ask.

She shuts it with her finger where she left off. "It's a book on how to love yourself."

I cock an eyebrow. "You don't love yourself?"

She puts the bookmark inside the book and places it in her lap, turning her body toward me. "I love myself, but this is teaching me how to keep toxic relationships at bay. Make positive lifestyle changes. Meditation. That sort of thing."

"Who's toxic?" I ask.

She tilts her head. "Aren't we nosy today?"

"I'm just curious. I'm not toxic, am I?"

"The fact that I'm willingly on a plane with you and that you bought me a first class seat and have a hotel room booked for me says you're not toxic." She moves to pick up her book, but I like having her attention, so I keep the conversation going.

"Is it Jeremy?" I wanted to ask her about her ex that night in Colorado, but she didn't seem to feel much like talking, so I walked her to her hotel room and said good night like a gentleman.

She sighs. "I knew you wanted details."

I shrug. "I find out you were dating a pro football

player after you tell me you don't date athletes. Of course I'm gonna want answers."

She studies me for a moment then sighs. "It's not an original story. We were high school sweethearts, ended up at the same college. He got drafted to Florida, and I followed him. He got traded to Wisconsin and told me he didn't want me to go with him. Apparently he wanted to spread his wings and live a little."

My brow furrows in irritation. "Why didn't he tell you that when you were in Idaho?"

"That's a question you'd have to ask him. So he left me in Florida, knowing no one but Tedi. Oh, and he was cheating on me. Tedi's the one who told me. We lived in the same apartment complex. So there's that too."

Fuck, no wonder she doesn't trust athletes.

"Well, it sounds like he's just a douche. You should give other athletes a chance." Her eyes narrow a bit and I raise my hands. "You know, if you and Joran don't work out."

Something falls over her face, but I can't decipher it at all, which is weird because usually I have a pretty good read on her nonverbal.

"You know how you say your profession might make it hard to find someone genuine who wants you as a person and not just everything that comes with you?" she asks.

I nod.

"Well, it's kind of the same but in reverse when you're dating an athlete. A lot of you guys are charismatic. Could sell a girl on anything, make her believe how special she is, but then the one night the girlfriend doesn't go out, some other girl is there telling you how great you are and you're eating it up. No offense, but I think athletes live and die by their egos."

I study her for a moment. Damn, Jeremy did a number on her. But it's not because he's an athlete. Look at Joran. I don't want to be the bearer of bad news, but he's a womanizer who's probably sleeping around on her and he's not an athlete.

"I know the kind of guys you're talking about, and maybe hockey is different, I don't know, but there're a lot of guys in the league who are happily married, have kids, are faithful. Ones who go to their hotel rooms and call their wives instead of going out to a bar. Ones who don't take every opportunity to sleep with any woman who's presented to them. It might be a small number, but there are good ones out there. Jeremy just wasn't a good one."

Her gaze falls to her lap. "Maybe so, but I'm not willing to take that chance after getting bulldozed the first time around."

"You're scared?"

She says nothing for a moment, but then her back goes straight and she picks up her book off her lap. "I'm not scared. I'm just logical."

She opens her book and I figure this conversation is over—for now.

———

*W*e check in, drop our bags in our rooms, and I get Saige to the rink with the promise of us doing some promo shots for her company. So far the social media thing hasn't been terrible, but I'm still worried that what happened before might happen again.

I'm thankful that the new skates I arranged for her are up in my room when I arrive, and I tuck the box into my hockey bag and bring it down to the lobby with me. I opted for figure skates because I didn't think she'd want hockey skates. Hopefully I made the right call. Saige is already there, looking through some brochures. Sadly, we won't have a lot of time to sightsee this trip, since we're going to my cousin's adoption party.

I lean in and whisper, "Miss me?"

She startles and steps back into my chest. "Why must you do that?"

"Because it's fun." I hold my arm out for her to go out of the hotel first.

The doorman hails us a taxi, and it doesn't take long for us to get to the arena. Once we're out, I follow the directions and ask security who I should talk to. Everyone is accommodating and gracious, and we're escorted to the ice as they pop on the lights. The entire arena is empty, and the Zamboni has just gone over it, so all we can see is the shine of smooth ice.

"These are the perks I enjoy." I stare at the fresh ice and inhale deeply. "It's beautiful."

Saige stares and huffs. "We don't share the same thought."

"Really? You don't find an ice rink, an empty ice rink, alluring?"

"Actually it makes me nauseous."

I think about the skates in my bag for her. Damn it. "Have you never skated before? Because I'm an excellent teacher."

She smiles, rolling her mesmerizing eyes. "I'm sure you are. Too bad I don't have any skates," she singsongs the last part.

"Au contraire." I unzip my bag and hold up the box of women's skates for her.

"You planned this?"

I shrug. "I knew I had it all to myself and you can watch me do drills and take pictures and videos, or we can skate together. I'd love to teach you."

She stares at the ice. "I'm not sure, what if I fall?"

"I'll catch you, but I won't let you fall."

"I could break something."

"Not with me here." I point at my chest as though I'm a superhero or something.

She giggles and hope fills me. "You have an answer for everything, don't you?"

"Pretty much." I grin.

She snags the box out of my hands and sits down to put them on. "You're responsible if something happens to me."

"Definitely."

My hands itch with the possibility of having them on her hips. Sometimes I feel as though I'm deceiving Joran because I have no idea what's going on with them, but she never speaks about him and I don't ask because I don't really want to hear about any of their dates. Most times I forget he's the other guy.

I've got my skates on first, so I head out to the ice and do a lap while she finishes lacing hers. I skid to a stop at the opening and find her walking around the black rubber floor, practicing her footing. I hold out my hand for her to take and she accepts it, her ankles getting more used to wearing skates.

"I haven't been on a pair of skates in a while," she says.

"Don't worry, you're safe with me," I say softly, bringing her out onto the ice.

While I pull her toward me, she keeps her legs straight and both skates together. "Like this?"

"Yep, now try to push off with one foot and glide forward on the other."

She tries it and gets it right away, then does it a few more times while I hold her hands and skate backward in front of her so I can watch.

"This is kinda fun. Can I try backward? That looks fun too."

I laugh. "Not yet. Let's master this way first."

She pouts playfully. If she were mine, her lips would be swollen and red all the time because I'm not sure I'd ever be done kissing her.

We skate around the rink another time and I'm impressed with how well she's taking to it. "You're a natural. I'm going to talk to Coach about getting you a spot on the team."

"Can I try skating backward now?"

"Sure. Let me put my hands on your hips to help guide you." My hands fall to her hips and I slow us so I can turn her around to skate backward.

"Hold on a second. Let me try on my own," she says.

"What?" My forehead wrinkles.

I take my hands off her hips and watch as she skates away—backward. I'm slack-jawed until she flies up into a double Axel and comes back down, her speed increasing as her hair flows behind her while she whips around the rink. She uses the toe pick to stop herself and grins at me.

I shake my head. "What the hell?"

"Sorry, I think you were hoping for a damsel in distress on the ice rink and I didn't want to disappoint you, but being back on ice does feel good." She skates away, switching back and forth between skating forward and back then twirling. She's magnificent. "I was an ice skater growing up. Never went anywhere with it though."

"I'm not sure why not. You're really good at it."

"Eh, you know how it is. Hard to break into and I eventually got tired of starving myself, getting up at four a.m., and being ridiculed on everything from performance to technique. I just wasn't invested enough to continue."

She comes to a stop in front of me. "But I'll tell you one thing I've never done on the ice."

"What's that?"

"Played hockey."

"You're kidding?"

She shakes her head. "Nope. When I figure skated, I hated the hockey players because they always felt like they deserved more ice time than us. Why do you think our practices always started at five a.m.?"

"See? And I was the hockey player more than willing to watch the ice skaters twirl around."

She narrows her eyes at me. "Is that all you thought we did was twirl around?"

I skate over to my bag to grab some sticks and pucks. "Hell no, I give you skaters props. To spin and land like that is scary shit."

"And to me, being plowed into by two hundred and ten pounds is scary shit."

I laugh and toss a puck on the ice and bring over one stick. I set us up with the puck and wrap my arms around her while we both hold the stick.

"You smell good," I murmur, fully aware I'm going half chub.

"Thank you," she says in a soft voice.

I rock the stick back then bring it forward, shooting the puck into the net.

She couldn't be more perfect for me if a mad scientist made her specifically for me. I feel my willpower waning and I'm not sure how this is going to pan out because I keep thinking, "Joran who?"

CHAPTER 16

"This could be addicting."

Saige

"$\mathscr{T}$hanks for that. I didn't realize how much I missed it," I say to Aiden when we reach our hotel rooms. For tonight, he'll be staying next door to me, but tomorrow after the game, he has to go share a room with Maksim.

"You said the smell of the ice made you feel nauseous."

"For a long time, it did. My parents wanted to put me in more competitions because some coach I was working with told them there was hope for me. I saw my competition out there on the ice every Saturday. Pretty sure the coach just wanted my parents' money." I use my key card and enter my room. Surprisingly, Aiden follows me. "I humored them for a while, but the criticism was intense and I started to hate going to practice, so eventually I faked an injury. Never really skated again… until today."

"You seemed to enjoy it. You're graceful."

I put my suitcase on the luggage holder and Aiden sits on the edge of the bed. "You're a hockey player, of course I seem graceful."

I laugh, but in truth, Aiden gave me something today he didn't plan to. He reminded me that I used to love skating. It's probably why I love watching him on the ice, although I act like I don't.

I say, "You proved to be a great friend again today."

"Perfect. That's what I'm striving for, to get stuck in the friend zone."

I ignore his comment because if he knew how much being in this hotel room with him unnerves me, he wouldn't joke about it. I need to remain strong. Eventually he'll waver and his attention will shift to someone else. I don't want to think about how I'll handle that when the time comes.

"How is Joran anyway?" he asks.

I freeze for a moment while unzipping my bag. "Good."

I don't want to lie, so I don't say anything more. I'm guessing Joran hasn't told Aiden about me ending things. It's been an easy way for me to keep Aiden in the friend zone without much pushback from him.

He stands abruptly. "Want to do dinner tonight? Or we could just hang in the room and watch a movie?"

Should I do any of this with Aiden? Hell no.

Should I politely decline? Of course.

Will I? Not a chance.

I guess I'm a glutton for punishment.

"I'm cool with whatever." I shrug.

"I'll make reservations. You know how I hate being stuck in the hotel room. Nothing too fancy." He heads toward the door.

"Sounds good."

"See you in a little bit… friend." He leaves and the door slams shut.

The walls are so thin, I hear him walk into his room beside mine. My body begs for me to quit this game. To go next door and tell him how much I yearn for him every night. But doing that would only double the heartbreak later. Seeing Jeremy proved that. If I couldn't figure out a man was using me for six years, how can I trust my gut after less than a couple months with another man?

Technically, Aiden hasn't made an advance on me. Flirtatious comments aren't actions. He could be a massive flirt like that with everyone for all I know.

I finish unpacking, trying to keep my mind off Aiden—which is impossible when I pull out my dress for tomorrow. My Florida Fury fan wear seems to keep on growing. My phone dings with a text from Aiden that says he'll pick me up at seven, dress casual.

Since I have a few hours, I set my computer on the desk and check on my clients' social media, but something catches my eye. I glance down at the garbage can and find my self-help book in the trash.

What the hell?

I pick it up and place it back on the table. It must have fallen in.

One thing I can say about Aiden is that he's always punctual. At seven on the dot, a knock sounds on my door and I leave the bathroom to let him in.

"Nice look," he says, much more chipper than he was earlier.

"Sorry, one more eyelash to go." I take the eyelash curler off the lashes on my right eye and move it to my left while I head back to the bathroom.

"No problem." He must go sit in the room while I finish with my makeup.

When I come out a few minutes later, he's thumbing through the self-help book.

"Did you by chance throw my book away earlier?"

"Yep," he answers and tosses it in the trash again. "You don't need that. You're perfect the way you are."

I pass him and grab the book out of the empty trash. "You can't just throw away my book, Aiden."

He shrugs. "Suit yourself then. You look great."

I'm only wearing a pair of jeans, a tight V-neck long-sleeved shirt, and I'll have a coat on until we get there. "You did say casual, right?"

He has on a pair of jeans and a V-neck sweater with nothing else, so I'm assuming I'm good.

"Yeah, you ready then?"

"I am."

I grab my purse and we leave the room, walking toward the elevator. "Do you think someone might recognize you with no hat and no sunglasses?"

"Probably. I hope it's not too annoying for you."

"Oh, I don't care. Don't ever do anything on account of me."

The elevator arrives and we step in. With only us, it feels intimate and somewhat like a date. When it dings on the bottom floor, Aiden takes my hand and leads me out of the elevator as though I'm his. I'm so busy inwardly sighing at how perfect it feels that I don't bother to pull away. God, I'm playing with fire here. I know it, but I can't seem to help myself.

A few people whisper and point, but we get through the lobby without anyone stopping us. There's a car out front and the doorman nods when he sees Aiden. "Mr. Drake, your ride is here."

We've always taken taxis, so I'm not sure what's up with this blacked-out SUV with a private driver thing.

"Just makes it easier in New York," Aiden says as though he's reading my mind and dismissing the car as anything important.

"For sure," I agree.

We get into the SUV and pull away from the hotel.

"Are you going to tell me where we're going?" I ask.

"Nope."

"Seriously?"

"Nope." He grins as though he's enjoying this.

So we sit in the car and I stare at the city that never sleeps. All the lights, the people milling around, it's addictive and makes me want to be a part of it. I kind of wish we could've walked to dinner, but maybe tomorrow. Once again, we're in a city in the north in February. I think California has a hockey team—why can't we go there?

The car slows and I look out the window to see we're outside a Mexican restaurant.

"I'll text you when we're ready after," Aiden tells the driver.

"Have fun," he says to us.

Aiden files out first and offers me his hand to step onto the curb. He doesn't wait around too long before he ushers us into the restaurant—I assume so no one recognizes him. It's as though he set up this whole thing because the hostess knows who he is and we don't have to wait with other patrons. We're taken immediately down a hallway.

"Are you kidnapping me?" I ask in jest.

He chuckles behind me. "Maybe one day, but today's not your lucky day."

I can't help but smile as we continue down the hall. I'm thankful it's so dim in here that he won't see my grin. I don't want to lead him on, but I can't deny that I enjoy our flirting.

The hostess stops in a back room that only holds about five tables. She says something quietly to a nearby waitress, who peers at us, then we're guided to a table in the back that has a curtain to keep us hidden from other guests.

One side is a booth and the other a chair, so I opt for the bench since I'm smaller. Aiden folds his big body into the chair, thanks the hostess, and accepts both of our menus, holding one out to me.

"Is this hockey god privileges or what?" I touch the curtain.

"The best thing about New York is if you want to be private and you have money, they make it happen." He looks over his menu as though this is nothing while I want to scream in delight. I've never felt so special.

I'd do well to remember that we are not on a date.

"This could be addicting," I whisper over the candles in the middle of the table.

Aiden glances around. "Trust me, this is one perk, but there're a lot of cons that come with the territory too."

"Like?"

"Like the hostess could be calling her friends to say that I'm here and I'll be bombarded with requests for autographs and tickets as soon as we walk out."

"So enjoy the moment, is what you're saying?"

He smiles, and his face in candlelight makes my ovaries squeeze. Damn, he's so good-looking.

"Enjoy the moment," he says in a husky voice that makes my panties wet.

Aiden goes on to tell me how he's been here before and that he loves the guacamole. He makes suggestions about what's good but doesn't try to pressure me on what to choose. I decide on the taco salad and he gets the carne asada. We both order margaritas and relax back into our seats.

"Thank you, this is really nice," I say.

"Really nice would've been a Michelin three-star restaurant, which I would've done. But this is what the friend zone gets you." His smile says he's not serious, but his comment makes me think that maybe I need to nip this in the bud.

"I sense that you're not thrilled about the friends thing?"

He straightens his napkin on his lap and plays with it for a moment, seeming to wrestle with something, before he meets my gaze. "I'm not. If it wasn't for Joran, I'd already have asked you out on a real date. That's probably a shitty thing to say when the guy is my agent, but it's the honest truth and I can't pretend it isn't. This is the best I can do with you still involved with him."

I swallow the golf-ball-sized lie in the back of my throat. I could tell him that Joran and I aren't anything anymore, but then I'd probably end up sleeping with him tonight. "Oh."

He holds up his hand. "I'm sorry, I know I'm stepping over the line. It's just…" He shakes his head. "Never mind, can we just enjoy tonight? Platonically?"

My shoulders slouch and I sip my too-big margarita, loving the salt rim. "Did I ever tell you how much I love salt?" I change the subject to move past this awkwardness.

"I bet I can beat you with my love for salt with the weirdest thing I put it on."

"Oh, you're a salt lover?"

He nods. "I am."

"I put it on watermelon."

"Amateur. Pizza?" he asks.

"You got me there. I've never had it on pizza."

He closes his eyes. "Get a sausage and onion and put salt and pepper on it. You'll end up thanking me."

"I'll have to try that. I put my ketchup in a pile on the side of my plate, then top it with salt, then dip my salt-covered fries in it." I give him a look that says, "Beat that."

"Tried it. Loved it."

As if someone orchestrated it, the guacamole arrives with the basket of chips. Usually I'd shy away from adding salt in case the other person doesn't want it, but Aiden picks up the salt shaker and dangles it in front of my face.

I smile. "Go ahead."

"Come on, you know you want to do it," he teases.

I snag it from his grasp and shake it onto the guacamole. "Chips too?"

"Um… yeah." He grins.

We both pick up a chip and dip it in the guacamole, and it's so frickin' good.

"Seriously, I could get naked and swim in that guacamole, it's so good."

For a moment I think I stunned him speechless, but he cracks up a second later, then chokes on a chip and has to grab his water to get it down. "You're full of surprises, Saige Fowler."

Our eyes catch over the candlelight and it's on the tip of my tongue to tell him I'm single and available. That Joran isn't in my life and even when he was, it wasn't serious and it was never physical. I'd do just about anything to jump over this table and lick the guacamole off his hard muscular body. But I don't because I'd do just about anything—except get over the fear of breaking my own heart.

"You amaze me too, Aiden Drake."

And it's the truth. This man isn't who I thought he was, and I'm honored to be in his presence and thankful I threw a drink in his face on New Year's Eve. I had no idea how boring my life was without him in it.

Aiden

*W*e opt to walk to the theater because it's not that far away and I've come to enjoy viewing a new city through Saige's eyes.

"Can I give you a disclaimer before we get to the movie theater?" I ask.

She smiles and gives a small wave to an elderly couple walking by. "Sure."

"I wanted to go to an older movie, but it's February, the month of love, so that means most movie theaters are playing romances. I found this one and they're showing 'bad boys and good girls' films. I couldn't pass it up. They're both Reese Witherspoon movies, so we have—"

"Oh, I like this already. I get to eat all the salt I want without feeling bad and then I get rom-coms? Best da—" She stops short. "Night ever."

"Just wait until you hear the movies. *Cruel Intentions* and *Fear*."

She chuckles. "Would you classify *Fear* as a romance?"

Other than knowing Mark Wahlberg is in it, I've never seen it. "I guess we'll discuss after."

"Why did you pick old movies?" she asks.

"I wanted to go somewhere with you where we

wouldn't be interrupted. Even if I can't talk to you, at least I'm not sharing you."

She stops walking on the sidewalk and looks at the ground. "Aiden…" There are tears in her eyes when she looks up.

"Don't make a big deal of it. Remember, I don't have a lot of friends." I grab her hand and tug her forward.

"That's the nicest thing anyone has ever said to me."

"It shouldn't be. Jeremy should've put you on a pedestal. Dumbass didn't, I guess."

The movie theater is across the street, so I lead her over to get our tickets before I embarrass myself further. Inside, we opt for no more food since we just finished dinner.

I let Saige pick our seats and she heads right to the middle, her decision speaking volumes about this being a platonic experience. If I don't shut my mouth soon, she's going to stop hanging out with me and I don't know if I could handle that right now. If the choice is for us to be friends or nothing, I'll pick friends.

There aren't a lot of other people in the theater and the ones who are here seem more into each other than what's playing on the screen. The lights dim and I slide down in my seat, spreading my knees wide and crossing my arms so I don't try to get handsy with Saige.

Fear comes on first and we sit through the movie, not saying much. She jumps a few times when Mark Wahlberg's character gives us a scare. I get what she's saying about this not being romantic.

"I'm gonna get a snack, want one?" I ask her.

"Anything chocolate," she whispers.

"Okay, I'll be back."

Leaving the theater, I exhale a deep breath. Being so close to her and not being able to touch her in any way is torture. I need to control these feelings. A good beat-off job tonight should suffice. For a little while anyway.

I leave the concession stand with Twizzlers and Peanut M&M's. I hope she's not allergic to peanuts. Surely I'd know that by now, right?

"Excuse me, Mr. Drake?" The guy who helped me at the concession stand stops me before I can leave. I knew he was overly nice to me.

"Yeah?"

"Could I get an autograph?" He holds out a napkin and pen.

"Sure." I set down the candy and scribble my signature.

"Thanks. I'll be at the game tomorrow night."

"Rooting for the home team?" I ask with a smile.

He nods enthusiastically. "Yeah."

"Good for you, but I hate to tell you… you might be disappointed tomorrow night."

He laughs and looks down the hall, then gets me a tub of popcorn. "On the house."

"You don't have to do that."

"You're, like, the only celebrity we've ever had in here. You're lucky the manager hasn't taken your picture to post in the lobby."

We both laugh and I walk away with a free popcorn and my candy.

The next movie is already starting by the time I rejoin Saige. I hand her the Peanut M&M's and she smiles, so I guess no nut allergy.

She eyes my popcorn and I hold it out to her. "Free popcorn. Another perk."

She laughs and a couple in the back row shh us. Not sure why—when I passed them, they were getting a helluva lot more action than I am.

We watch *Cruel Intentions* and if I thought the sex scenes in *Fear* were bad, this is downright blue ball material. The fact that I won't be getting any when I head back to the hotel is forefront in my mind after watching this.

The movie ends and I swear I deserve some sort of medal for not even putting my arm on the back of her chair. We follow the other guests out of the theater and it's then I see a crowd of people outside. I cup Saige's elbow and pull her back into the theater, down the aisle, and out the door that says Exit. The door slams shut behind us and we're left in an alley.

"I guess that whole 'alarm will sound' thing is a joke," she says.

I put my finger over my lips and take her hand, escorting her up the alley to the front of the theater. I peek around the corner, and as I assumed, it's the fucking paps and a bunch of women, a few men scattered in. Saige looks and turns back to me with an open mouth and wide eyes. She pulls out her phone and hops on social media, then shows me that I was tagged at the movie theater by none other than the free popcorn guy. I should've just played the look-alike card.

I text the driver to meet me on the next corner over. Once he messages back that he's waiting, I lead Saige down the sidewalk away from the theater. I usher her into the car and the paps just figure it out when I climb in and lock the doors.

"And that's the con I was telling you about." My lips are a thin line.

Saige looks out the back window of the car. "The women are running, screaming out to you, but I can't hear them."

"Just turn around," I say.

She eventually does face forward after we turn the

corner and lose the crowd.

"Man, I've never experienced something like that before." She leans back. "What do you think would've happened if they got to us?"

"Well, first they would've tried to figure out who you are, then reports of us dating would hit the fan sites and they probably would've smeared your name. Oh yeah, and we'd have some explaining to do to Joran. Not that we've crossed any lines, but you know what I mean. It doesn't look good."

She stares out the window, not saying anything.

I touch her knee. "Sorry I spoiled the mood."

What I keep to myself is that I'm bothered she can't be mine. I'm pissed that I couldn't take her hand and walk out of that theater with her, proud to say she's my girl. And it's not only because she's with Joran, but also the fact that she'd be ridiculed by the female fans. They'll point out everything they perceive as a flaw as though they're perfect specimens. I've seen it time and time again. I don't even want to think of what male fans might say. I have no idea if that's something she's willing to put herself through, but considering that she hated the way she was constantly criticized while skating, I can't imagine she'd want to endure public scrutiny.

The driver stops in front of the hotel entrance, and we file out of the car and into the lobby. Without stopping, we go straight to the elevator and I ask her if she wants to come to my room for a nightcap.

"I probably shouldn't," she says, lingering by her door.

This is the first time she's turned me down and I can't lie, it hurts. "Just one."

She shakes her head. "I had a lot of fun tonight. Thank you."

If I were a lesser man, I'd tell her the fun doesn't have

to be over. That I could show her a thing or two about fun in my room.

I shift my weight. "You're welcome. So we have to be at the courthouse around eleven tomorrow."

"I'll be ready."

"Great. And just so you know, my cousin, Frankie… she's kind of outspoken."

She nods. "Must be a family trait."

"I suppose so." I nod for her to open the door. "Don't be up late reading that bullshit self-help stuff, okay?"

She uses her key card, and the green light makes me inwardly groan that this is the end of our night. The end of my time with her. "I'll probably just pull out my vibrator after that movie."

I freeze and blink a few times. "You didn't just say that."

"Oh, come on, I saw you shifting in your seat during that scene where Reese and Ryan make love."

She's right, I was. "Actually I was thinking about that scene in *Fear* when they're on the roller coaster. I'd love to do that sometime."

Her cheeks flush pink. I need to cut this off now if my dick's gonna survive the beating I'll need to give it to satisfy myself after this conversation.

"Well, good night, Saige. If you need me, I'm right next door."

Our eyes lock and I'm ashamed of myself for almost begging her to accept my invitation for a drink.

"Good night, Aiden," she says, and I wait for her door to shut.

My empty hotel room has never felt as lonely as it does tonight, especially knowing Saige is on the other side of the wall. She could be taking off those skintight jeans or the bra that hugged her tits so perfectly. Does she sleep naked, or does she have a matching silk set that shows how hard her nipples get?

I drop to the bed, kicking off my shoes and begging my mind to stop torturing me, but the visions keep coming and I can't stop them. What she looks like under those layers of clothes. How sweet she must look when she comes. The pleas that might come from her mouth if I denied her an orgasm.

I undo my belt and open my jeans, pulling my half-hard length out of my boxer briefs. I tug and pull and pump, allowing my imagination to take me where I'm not allowed—into her bed. Feeling her thighs quiver as I settle between them and watching her back arch when my tongue slides up her folds and circles her clit. The soft purrs falling from her lips as I knead her breasts and pinch her nipples.

"Fuck," I mumble, pumping my dick faster.

Now she's riding me and I'm on my back, watching her tits bounce while she teases me. I slide in and out of her in a glorious, painstakingly slow motion. Needing more, I flip her over to take control, drilling into her as she tightens her thighs around my waist.

I imagine her saying, "Fuck me, Aiden. Harder, harder. That's it. Damn, you're so good. We're fucking perfect together."

I come with a jolt, and a spray of my semen lands all over my shirt. My dick convulses in my hand and I'm unable to stop jerking as more and more of my seed pours out.

Once I think I'm done, I lie on the bed, sprawled out, wishing it wasn't just my imagination. How long do I want to do this to myself? I'm clearly getting nowhere here—I'm not getting over her and I can't get under her. What the hell's a guy to do?

"Mind if I keep my bag in your room."

Aiden

I'll admit it, the next day, I'm in a pissy mood from the moment I wake up. Actually, from the time I went to bed after having to jerk off when I should've been deep inside Saige. My frustration level at not being able to pursue Saige outright is at its highest point yet.

Now I sit in the courthouse about an hour outside of the city, watching my cousin, Frankie, with her husband as he adopts her daughter, Jolie. Frankie's had a rough life. Jolie's father was a shithead addict who'd get rough with Frankie. She doesn't talk about it much and I'm sure I've only gotten part of the story, but needless to say, it wasn't a healthy relationship. She got out and found Jax, who is an awesome guy and loves Jolie like his own. Now Frankie's pregnant with Jax's kid and they're living that happily ever after most people assume they will get at some point.

I always figured my time for that would come when I'm not playing anymore.

"She's adorable," Saige whispers next to me, her eyes on Jolie.

I nod and she crosses her legs the opposite way of me.

After the family hugs and everyone claps, we file out of the courthouse, where all their friends wish them congratulations.

"Hey, Frankie," I say and kiss her cheek. "This is Saige."

Jolie runs up and catches my legs. "Aiden, did you see?"

Jax joins us and I shake his hand, congratulating him, while Frankie tries to give Saige the third degree.

I squat down to Jolie's height. "So you're an Owens now, huh?"

She smiles proudly and nods.

"I think that's pretty awesome."

"I know." She wraps her arms around my neck. "And I'm having a baby brother," she whispers.

I high-five her and pick her up. "Coolest big sis ever."

"We're coming to see you tonight, right?" Jolie asks.

"That's the plan," I say, glancing behind me to see Saige now talking with Jax and some of his friends. She's explaining what position I play and pretty much bragging about me. I can't say it doesn't put a smile on my face.

"I can't wait. Jax let me stay up and watch a game the other night. One guy slammed this other guy into the boards."

"Jax, you letting Jolie watch hockey?" She nods. "Guess what?" I whisper.

Jolie takes her hands and puts them and her lips at my ear. "What?"

"Saige used to figure skate." I tell her this to endear Saige to her, but her face twists.

"Hockey's better."

I squeeze Jolie and throw her in the air. "You know it. I'll make you the best damn center in the game."

"She wants to be goalie," Jax says, coming over.

I stop in my tracks as we hit the bottom of the stairs outside. "Goalie?"

"Yeah. They get to wear those fun helmets and do the splits." Jolie's eyes are wide.

Jax clamps a hand down on my shoulder. "I tried to tell her."

"All they do is stop the puck. You want to be able to race around people, steal the puck, shoot the puck, and get the glory when you score."

"I like their gloves too," she says.

Jax laughs, stealing her from my arms. "That's what I love about you. One-track mind just like your mama." Jax nuzzles his face into hers and kisses her cheek.

Jolie draws back as we reach the parking lot. "I'll give you today, but then only kisses at night. I'm getting old."

We all laugh and file into the cars to head to the luncheon. None of our family from Wisconsin came because it's hard for them to get off.

"Your mom sent the most beautiful arrangement," Frankie says from the front seat.

Saige and I are wedged in the back with a child seat and Jolie's wiggling body between us.

"And cheese curds," Jolie says.

Frankie and I are distant from our parents in our own ways, although Frankie much more than me. She ran away young and met Jolie's father. Her parents didn't approve, and when they don't approve, you don't do it. Frankie did it without caring. I hope one day they'll bridge that gap, but truthfully, I don't blame her if she doesn't.

"Tell me your mom knows how to make them for you?" I ask.

Frankie points at me. "Shut your mouth. I taught you how to make them."

We pull up to a restaurant called The Porterhouse. Once we're all out of the car, Jolie takes my hand and one of Saige's. We lift her and she giggles. Our eyes catch over Jolie's head, and for some weird reason, I see a vivid flash of myself in the future doing just this. I shake the thought from my head because that's ridiculous.

We find our seats in the restaurant and order our drinks. Jax and Frankie disappear into the bathroom for a bit, and I get the distinct feeling they're getting it on. Saige carries on a conversation with the other people at the table. The more time that passes, the sourer I get.

"You okay?" Saige whispers in my ear.

"I'm fine. Just didn't sleep well last night."

She cringes a bit. "Hotel beds."

"Sure, that's it."

Frankie and Jax finally return to the table and the meal is served.

Frankie looks at my plate. "Why aren't you having a steak?"

She'll think this is pathetic, but I tell her how I decided to have the same thing I ate before the last game since I had two goals *and* two assists.

What the hell has happened to me? I used to have inherent luck. Hell, I was the guy who didn't balk at wearing jersey number thirteen, and now I'm loading up on superstitions.

"You really think that's going to make a difference?" Frankie asks.

"Dunno. But I have to perform. Trade deadline is in a few weeks."

"Trade deadline?" she asks because she doesn't know anything about hockey.

Saige nods. She's probably crossing the days off on her calendar for when she can be rid of me. *Too bad you're stuck with me for the whole season, sweetheart.*

"The last day they can trade me."

"Aiden, you're doing awesome. You've been a scoring machine," Jax says.

I sip my water and nod. "Because I've been adhering to the superstitions—"

"The only good thing is that he doesn't synchronize all his meals with a time," Saige says.

I glance at her and smile. I start to extend my arm around the back of her chair, but I stop myself halfway and tuck my hand under the table.

"You really believe in all that?" Frankie asks.

"I didn't until I fell into the slump of all slumps."

"How do you know Saige isn't your lucky charm?" she asks with a grin.

I devour the rest of my sandwich, swallowing with a big gulp of water. "She is."

"Oh, that's sweet," Frankie says, looking at Jax.

"It's not what you think," Saige says, shifting in her seat and looking a little uncomfortable.

Frankie's forehead wrinkles. "I don't understand."

I check my watch and wipe my mouth. "I have to get to the stadium." I raise my hand at the server.

"You should take a steak to go and have it after the game. You'll probably be starving," Jax says.

The server comes over and sets down a glass of white wine like I'd arranged for earlier. I slide it over to Saige.

"Ready?" she asks.

"You don't have to ask me that every time." I put my arm on her chair and she briefly narrows her eyes at me.

"Fine." She tosses the wine in my face.

Frankie gasps while it drips down my face, and everyone else in our private room stares at us.

"I was just being polite." Saige shrugs. Seems my mood is rubbing off on her.

"I know. Sorry. Thanks though." I wipe my face with a napkin and drop it on the table. "See you all tonight."

I stand and Saige follows suit.

"Aiden," Frankie says, standing and stopping me. "What—"

I place my hand on her shoulder. "She throws a drink in my face before every game for good luck. Long story." I bend over and kiss Frankie's cheek. "See you tonight. Tickets are at will call."

"Thank you for having me. Lovely ceremony and family." Saige touches Frankie's hand and I pick up my wrist to look at my watch.

We head back to the hotel, where I have to pack my bags and head down to Maksim's room.

At our doors, I ask, "Mind if I keep my bag in your room until after?"

"You're paying the bill. It's your room." She uses her key card to enter her room while I go in mine.

"I'll be over soon."

My room is quiet, and my bag is already packed except for the suit I have to change into and the clothes I wore today. Watching my cousin have her happily ever after was awesome but gut-wrenching at the same time. I always told myself I'd be cool to wait to find my person until my career was over. Having a serious relationship while trying to be at the top of your profession is an impossible feat. Both require dedication and focus, and there's only so much time and effort a person has to give.

Then Saige comes skipping along into my life and nothing seems as important as her, even my hockey career. I'm on the cusp of greatness in my field, could get a contract at the end of this year that would set records, and my mind is all tangled up in my feelings for a woman. A woman who doesn't have any interest in me because I'm an athlete. Not that it matters because she's already seeing someone. And I know something weird is going on with her and Joran because why is he never around? If they're together, how can the bastard treat her like this?

I take two Advil because my head hurts from thinking about this frustrating situation I find myself in. I change into my suit, add the clothes I was wearing to my suitcase, and knock on her door. Rather than hanging out for the ten minutes I have left, I decide to leave right away.

"Thanks. Your ticket's at will call. I have you next to Frankie. I hope that's okay?" I say with the hotel door open.

She nods and slides to the end of the bed, her bare feet having small indentations from the heels she wore. Her nails are painted a bright red, which only makes me think of sex. Sex with her. Sex right now on that bed.

"See you tonight." I shut the door and take a moment to breathe before heading to the elevator. The one good thing is my room won't be right next to hers tonight.

Saige

I find my seat, which is in the first row as usual. Frankie, Jax, and Jolie are already seated with enough stuff from the concession stand to feed a small army. This is uncomfortable, especially since Aiden was acting like a bit of a class-A asshole today. I'm not sure why he woke up on the wrong side of the bed, but I hope he changes.

"Hi," I say to Frankie and sit down next to her with my Diet Coke and popcorn.

"This is so exciting," she says.

The guys are all on the ice, warming up. I purposely delayed my arrival because Aiden normally doesn't have his helmet on during warmups and it gets me way more turned on than it should.

Jolie and Jax are at the glass and Aiden winks at them every time he skates by. Even Maksim and Ford tap the ends of their sticks to the glass as they pass by.

"Do you know Maksim and Ford?" I ask Frankie.

"Yeah, the three of them came out when Jax and I were doing a tattoo pop-up in Vegas. Funny guys."

"That's for sure."

I knew Jax and Frankie are both tattoo artists, but I forgot that Jax is well known in the circuit, according to

Aiden. I guess Frankie has been gaining more traction since they've been together too.

I concentrate on eating my popcorn, trying not to pay attention to Aiden, but it's like having a vulture circling and not double-checking where it is at all times.

"Aiden said you're handling his social media now," Frankie says.

I know she's trying to be polite and make conversation. Any other day, I'd be up for it. But the way things were left with Aiden today, I can't seem to pick myself up. I hate this distance between us.

"I do. I throw a drink in his face and he allows me to use him as an endorsement for my company. Works for us," I say.

"That says a lot about you... that he'd trust you with that. After everything."

I tilt my head, and when I say nothing else, she glances over, stopping and holding my gaze with wide eyes.

"You don't know." She blows out a breath. "Shit. Forget I said anything."

The hairs on the back of my neck stand up. "Frankie..."

She's got to be kidding me. Aiden is so closed off. I tried to find out why he cut himself off of social media, but I found nothing.

She shakes her head. "It's not anything I'm at liberty to talk about. I'm sorry."

I sit up straighter as the warmups end. Aiden says goodbye to Jolie with a wave of his glove, his gaze lingering on me briefly. He skids to a stop, staring at Frankie and me. The smile that glowed on his face a second ago fades.

I wave to him and give him a thumbs-up for luck. Eventually Ford slaps him on the back, and Aiden moves along.

"Please," I beg her.

Frankie looks at her cousin, who's with his teammates. "You didn't hear it from me."

"Okay."

"Aiden has an older sister, Connie, and she has a daughter, Emma. She's always been Aiden's biggest fan. Aiden's sister is ten years older than him, so she had Emma when he was only fifteen. When Aiden got drafted to the national league, Emma bragged about him to anyone who wanted to hear. Her parents let her get on social media to keep track of him and, let's face it, to make Emma happy."

I have no idea what this has to do with him going off social media, but I listen on.

"Emma joined some fan groups and let it out that she was Aiden's niece. It took Aiden a while to find his footing and people told Emma what they thought about her uncle. None of it was good. Emma got defensive, but she was a twelve-year-old playing with grown adults and teens. They were so mean the way they bullied and belittled her... some of the things they would say." Frankie shakes her head and looks at me, sadness coating her features. "You know how it is when the mob on social media attacks... in the end, she tried to take her life."

My hand flies to my mouth with a gasp and my heart sinks to my stomach. I search out Aiden on the ice. He's skating to the face-off.

"Is she okay?"

Frankie nods. "Yeah, but Aiden took himself off social media. The entire family went off. You can imagine how traumatic it was for them."

I sink back into my seat. The fact that he allowed me to get him back on social media, to have him as my primary spokesperson with his name and image, after all his family went through... why would he agree to that?

She squeezes my knee. "That's why I was saying he must really trust you, which I think is great."

"Okay, you two, stop the talking. Aiden's about to win this face-off," Jax says, leaning over us.

Sure enough, Aiden wins and passes it to Ford. The two skate down the ice, and one of the players checks Aiden into the boards. Tweetie checks that guy and ties him up on the boards, so Aiden skates away. Ford passes Aiden the puck and he rushes toward the goal.

"Go, Aiden!" Jolie screams at the glass.

He does some fancy stick move and shoots it into the top corner of the net. All his teammates rush over and congratulate him. Aiden gets the puck, bouncing it on his stick, and tosses it over the partition to Jolie. Jax is able to grab it before the guy behind him gets his paws on it.

"Asshole," Frankie murmurs.

I shake my head at the guy behind us who tried to take the puck from a little girl. Jolie hugs the puck as if it's a stuffed animal. She really is the cutest girl I've ever seen.

Aiden's on fire the rest of the game. When he's on the ice, he's never far away from the puck. I try to spend some time on my phone so I don't seem too interested in the game. I'm sure Frankie senses something, and she would be bold enough to ask me what's going on between Aiden and myself. The last person I need to divulge all my complicated feelings regarding Aiden to is his cousin. *Hello, I'm Saige and I'm scared to date your cousin because I had this boyfriend in high school who fucked me up in the head and I can't seem to get out of the wicked tornado of unpleasant thoughts he put me in.*

The game ends with Aiden scoring the game-winning goal.

"I forgot what a great skater he is," Frankie says to me.

"I heard he's really good," I lie because I know how great of a skater he is.

"You don't watch all his games?" Frankie asks.

"I don't usually go to the games. But since he paid for my plane ticket and got me here, well, here I am." Again, I find myself lying just so she doesn't ask any more questions. I've been to every single game since I met Aiden.

Jax and Jolie scream and stand.

"He scored. We won!" Jax yells and they bang on the glass again.

Aiden winks, skating toward them. The crowd aws when he presses his hand to Jolie's through the glass.

"You two aren't together?" Frankie asks out of the blue.

See? This is why I was vague, but she's got those damn mom instincts.

I shake my head. "Nope. I'm just the girl who throws a drink in his face before a game."

I glance at the ice as his teammates all congratulate him. Our eyes lock briefly before I divert mine back to my phone.

*J*olie's exhausted after the game, so Frankie and Jax say good night after Aiden comes out of the locker room.

When Aiden and I get into our taxi to head back to the hotel, I say, "They're great people."

"Yeah, I'm super happy for her." His knee bounces beside me. Maybe he's still in a mood from before, though he had an amazing game, so I'm not sure why.

"You had a great game," I say to break the silence.

"Oh, you noticed?" There's irritation in his tone that I don't appreciate.

"What does that mean?"

"Every time I looked over, you were on your phone."

"And? Did I miss the part in our agreement where I had to cheer you on?" Anger is laced in my own voice and I hate it. We've never been this way with each other.

"Oh, so what do you want, a contract?"

The taxi stops outside the hotel. Aiden hands the driver some cash and opens the door. This time he doesn't hold out his hand for me. There are paps and crowds of women outside the hotel, and we've arrived at the same time as the bus of players. I don't know why Aiden didn't ride with his teammates if he was going to be this way with me.

Women are screaming and calling the names of all the players. Camera flashes go off and it's all a little disorienting.

"Drake!" Ford calls. "Captain!"

The team obviously started celebrating in the bus. Aiden walks over and I can tell that the guys are on cloud nine after their win. Some of the players wander over to the women, and they welcome a few of them to join them inside the hotel.

I roll my eyes and walk into the lobby. Whatever, I don't care what the hell he does.

I'm waiting for the elevator when Aiden comes up behind me. I know it's him because he's so close I can smell his cologne. A few other players I don't know wait with us, but they're too occupied with the giggling women who are all over them.

"We're heading to the bar on the top floor. Interested?" one guy asks Aiden.

"Maybe in a bit."

We all step into the elevator, but more players pile in, leaving me in the back corner with Aiden at my back. His hands steady me, holding my hips, and my back ends up pressed to his chest. It's all too much. I feel overwhelmed, like I'm suffocating. His fingers flex on my hips and his mouth comes down close to my ear.

"I'm sorry," he whispers, though he could probably talk normally and no one would hear him since these guys are so loud. "Forgive me for being a dick?"

His hot breath on my neck stirs all the sexual tension between us, stokes the glowing embers into a steady flame. My body feels wound tight and the space between my thighs tingles with anticipation and need.

I look over my shoulder and he's right there, his light stubble on his cheek scraping mine. "Why were you acting like that?"

"Because I want you so bad I can't see straight. I want you under me, over me, in the shower, bent over the bed. Any way I can get you. Do you really not see that?"

I say nothing, my breathing heavy, my gaze locked with his. His hands slide up under the hem of my Fury sweatshirt and he grabs the weight of my heavy breasts in each hand. My body gives in and I fall back against him, allowing him to do what he wants in this elevator filled with his teammates.

His mouth comes down on my neck and he licks his way up to my earlobe. "Tell me you want me too."

I remain silent and he pinches my nipples as though he doesn't accept that as an answer. My back arches, an invitation for him to continue, but the elevator stops. Aiden's hands slowly slide down and off my body.

A few players get out, saying they'll see everyone at the bar. That leaves us with the guys who picked up the puck bunnies.

"Maybe we'll see you up there," one guy says, his hand blatantly on the ass of the woman he just met.

"Yeah, maybe," Aiden answers and adjusts himself behind me right before the elevator stops on my floor. "I have to get my bag and head down to Maksim's room anyway. Maybe later."

He nudges me to step out of the elevator. Once we're both out, I start to walk down the hall, but he grabs my hand and tugs me back, caging me against the wall.

"Answer the question, Saige."

I look at him, desperate to feel those hands on me again. So I finally do what I've wanted to since I met him. I give in.

"I do," I answer.

"You do what?" He doesn't lay one finger on me and my skin burns to feel his touch once more.

"I want you, Aiden. I want you so bad it aches."

His mouth descends on mine and his tongue slides in. I lose all control, my hands rising and linking behind his neck. I'm ready to be his sex slave.

He strips his mouth off of mine. "Not here. I want you all to myself." Then he's dragging me down the hallway.

I put the key card on the lock and the green light is like a flashing go sign because Aiden opens the door, leads me inside, and slams it shut seconds before my back is against the wall again. His hands are on either side of my face while those eyes of his practically devour me.

God, I'm so screwed.

Saige

His mouth captures mine in a mix of passion and dominance. My hands fall behind me, trying to grip a wall with no edges.

"I've waited forever for this," he mumbles. His mouth falls to my neck as he turns my head in the direction he wants. Lifting my sweatshirt, he pulls it up over my head with my help, then presses my hands to the wall above my head. "Stay there."

His head nuzzles my tits in my cami. Once he feels I won't betray him and move my hands, he inches my cami up and over my tits, leaving the fabric to lay just above them. Falling down my body, Aiden massages my tits, sucks my nipples, and buries his face between them.

"Please," I beg, needing more.

Aiden finally lifts the cami completely off of me. "What do you want? Tell me."

He falls to his knees in front of me, unbuttoning my jeans and tugging them down my legs. I kick off my shoes and he takes off one sock at a time before wrangling my jeans down and off my body. Leaving me naked. He stares at my center with hunger in his eyes.

Before I can blink, his hands grab my ass, pulling me off the wall a bit so he can bury his face between my legs.

He inhales while I watch him with a pulsing need to feel his tongue on me. He doesn't disappoint, sucking my clit into his mouth. He raises his hand and smacks my ass, spurring me to arch and offer myself to him.

He brings one leg over his shoulder and manipulates my pussy with his mouth before drawing back and inserting his middle finger inside me. He watches himself move in and out while my head falls to the wall. He's a master at this. Throwing his suit coat off, he leaves it on the floor, burying his head in my pussy again while his finger continues to glide in and out of me.

"Right there. Don't stop," I pant, my breathing labored. Never did I think I'd be here with Aiden Drake right now. How did I ever deny myself him in the first place?

He takes me over the edge and my one hand strays, falling down to grip his hair as I shamelessly grind against his face. But his groans tell me he doesn't care, he's enjoying every bit of this, which only brings my orgasm to the brink faster.

"Oh god," I murmur, coming with a jolt before a pulsing wave flows through my body.

Damn, he's good. Better than good.

Climbing my body, his mouth covers mine and I taste myself on his tongue. My fingers manipulate his clothes, getting his tie and dress shirt off, then working on his pants. He toes out of his dress shoes and working as a team, we get him naked. He guides us to the bed, him sitting on the edge and me standing between his legs.

"You're too beautiful of a man," I say, my hands running down both his cheeks and staring down into his molten eyes.

His smoldering gaze doesn't break from mine. "You're the beautiful one." His hands wind around my body and grab my ass, pushing me toward him. "Are you okay?"

I nod and my forehead falls to his. "I'm great."

Which is true. We stand there like that, neither one saying a word, until the desire to have one another becomes too all-consuming.

His hands glide down my thighs, urging me to straddle him, and when I do, I'm rewarded with his length pressing into my folds. I grind along it and my arousal peaks again. He pulls me into his chest, and my nipples rub his hard pecs.

He says my name on a breath and I close my eyes. Hearing my name in such a different way from his lips feels almost overwhelming. As though I'm a fragile doll he's protecting.

"Yeah?" I mumble, still grinding against his hard heat.

"Are you clean?"

I draw back.

He looks a little nervous. "I'm tested all the time and I've never not used a condom. But whatever makes you comfortable is cool."

"I have an IUD and I don't dare tell you the last time I had sex, but needless to say it was a long time ago."

He smooths out my hair and tucks it behind my ear. "That makes me happy to hear."

"Well, it might take a while for me to find my rhythm again." I rise up on my knees.

"You sure about this?" He positions the tip of his cock at my opening.

My answer is to sink down on his length, letting him fill me.

"Damn," he whispers. "You feel fucking fantastic."

And so does he, but I can't find the words. I wrap my arms around his head, my fingers threading through his hair to ground him to me, as I ease his girth in and out of me. The stretch and fill of him is the stuff wet dreams are made of, and I moan.

He pushes up inside me and we find the perfect rhythm. "Never enough." His teeth scrape along the skin of my collarbone. "I'll never get enough of you."

I close my eyes and say a silent prayer that it's the truth, that he's not just feeding me a line, because I've never felt more connected to someone during sex than right now. It feels as though we were two lost puzzle pieces who found each other in a land of misfits. My arms tighten and his do the same, our lower halves doing the majority of the work. He grunts and I moan when he hits me so deep, it feels as though I might spontaneously orgasm.

"Aiden."

"Say it again," he orders.

"Aiden." My voice is breathy from the vibrating desire coursing through my body.

"You're amazing. I'm so fucking sorry for being a dick today," he says against my skin.

"It's fine."

He stops moving and waits for me to look at him. "It's never okay for me to be that way with you."

I nod. "Fine. Just don't stop again."

He chuckles and we pick up where we were, but now our paces speed up. He's pushing into me and I'm clenching around him. The overwhelming pleasure hits me fast, catapulting me over the edge Aiden had me teetering on.

"There you go," he says, and he buries his head into my neck, driving into me. "Fucking hell." He pumps into me once more before stilling inside me. His lips continue to kiss me as he fills me up. "So damn good."

He tilts my head so I can stare at him and we both smile.

Oh my god, I screwed Aiden Drake from the Florida Fury. Although to me, he just feels like Aiden.

I wake up to a phone buzzing, and I stir in Aiden's arms. At some point we must have fallen asleep. For a man who played an entire game of hockey, he had more stamina than I expected.

"It's mine," he says and gets out of bed to look for his slacks.

I sprawl out on my stomach, my head on the pillow, and glance at the clock. It's just after midnight, so we haven't been asleep long.

He answers his phone. "What?"

There's a short pause.

"You're kidding me. What time is it?"

Another pause.

"Don't worry about where I am."

Another pause.

"How the fuck did he let this happen? Jesus Christ. Give me ten."

He hangs up and crawls back up on the bed. "I have to go." He swipes my hair away from my face and kisses the nape of my neck. "I'll be back as soon as I can."

"Where do you have to go?" I ask, turning around to face him. I open my arms and he slides on top of me, the sheet the only barrier between us.

"Ford got in trouble," he says. "I forgot this is his hometown. Some woman is accusing him of fathering her child."

My eyes open in surprise. "Woah!"

"It's probably not true. You know how many guys I know who have been told they're gonna be daddies only to find out surprise, it's not theirs?" The bitterness in his tone grates on my nerves slightly. "But Ford has a hard time keeping it in his pants, so who knows." He dips down and kisses me softly. "I'll try to be back soon though."

"Okay." I rise up and kiss him one more time. It's addicting now that I know what his lips feel like. One kiss is like eating only one fun-size candy bar—never going to happen that it's enough.

"I'm going to turn on the light to find some clothes in my suitcase."

"Okay." I roll over.

His weight is soon off the bed, the bathroom light on, and I hear the zipper of his suitcase. I somehow move in and out of sleep while he gets ready, but with one last kiss, he's out the door and I fall back asleep.

I'm awoken with light streaming in through the curtains and my phone ringing on the nightstand.

"You little puck bunny!" Tedi screeches in my ear when I answer.

I sit up in bed, pulling the sheet to cover myself. "What are you talking about?"

"You really need to be more discreet."

"Back up about ten paces and start over. You've lost me."

"It's funny, I thought Aiden was a smart guy, but turns out he doesn't realize that the elevators in the hotel are glass… meaning people can see through them."

My mind travels back to last night on the elevator. There's no way anyone saw anything. We were packed like sardines.

"His lips on your neck and hands up your shirt ring a bell?"

"What?" I clutch the sheet to my chest tighter.

"Some paps got a video and you've been outed. They've already figured out who you are."

I get up off the bed and grab my laptop. "OMG, Tedi!"

I put her on speaker and move out of my phone app to search Aiden's social media because surely someone would comment on there or tag him in the video.

"You're not the first," Tedi says.

But I don't find anything, which is odd. Plus, wouldn't Aiden have figured that out already and called me? Then I realize who I'm dealing with.

"This is a joke. Tweetie saw and told you, didn't he?"

"Yep. But it should make you more cautious, my dear." She laughs manically. "But way to go on boning Aiden Drake. Finally! Now. Give me all the details."

"All you need to know is yes, he's good, which I'm sure you expected." I head into my texts to see if there's anything there and find one from Aiden from the middle of the night.

I guess he's still helping to clear things up with Ford's parents and their PR rep, putting a plan together. He and Maksim are staying for moral support because Ford's dad is being an asshole, but he'll come by afterward.

"Well, I'm sure he's no Tweetie, but I'm glad you finally got some. Where is he? Lying next to you? Please don't tell me his head is between your legs right now."

"Tedi! Get your mind out of the gutter. He had to run out."

"Oh." The excitement in her voice fades.

"What does that mean?"

"Like, after you had sex with him, he had to run out?"

I get what she's saying, but she has it all wrong. "He

told me why, I just can't tell you. It's legit. Not for cigarettes or something."

"Unless it was for more condoms, his ass should be in that bed with you."

If I could tell Tedi, she'd understand, but I can't at this point. It's Ford's business. "Let it go."

"I don't like it," she says.

"You don't have to. I do."

She sighs. "Anyway, I hate to be the bearer of bad news here, but what exactly did you tell him? Doesn't he think you're still dating Joran?"

Oh shit.

"Um…" I completely forgot about that.

She laughs again. "I love this. Your love life is always better than mine."

"I'll just tell him it's over and that will be it."

"Okay, and on your way back from fairy tale land, can you grab some of Rapunzel's hair so I can remain youthful?"

"I gotta go," I tell her and hang up because her sarcastic attitude isn't helping, plus she's putting doubts in my head about Aiden.

I try to shake it off, hoping Aiden returns soon. The longer he's away, the more I'm starting to feel like an actual puck bunny.

CHAPTER 21

Aiden

"*I* finally get her, and you drag me out of bed for this." I slide into Ford's car outside the hotel. He's obviously been home since he's driving his Aston Martin.

Maksim's in the back, looking about as comfortable as an elephant on a life raft.

"You do know you're a fucking hockey player, right? Couldn't you buy something that fits your size?" I try to stretch out my legs but there's not enough room.

I don't even have my seat belt on before Ford slams on the gas. "My dad's ready to have my ass and make me work for the family business. This is the last straw. If this is legit and I have a public pregnancy with some one-night stand." He shakes his head.

"I told you condoms are your friends," Maksim says from the back seat.

All I can think about is how I just had sex without a condom with Saige, a woman I've only known for a couple of months. But then I relax because this is Saige I'm talking about. I trust her.

"We've all been here, right?" Ford says, needing to make himself feel better.

Ford lives his life with reckless abandon. He doesn't

think of consequences and lives in the moment. Sometimes I think it's because he was born wanting nothing except a hockey career. Once he got that, it almost made him feel untouchable.

"Can't say I have. You, Mak?"

Maksim groans. "Can we please just get there? I can't feel my fucking legs."

"Come on, guys. What am I gonna do? A baby?" Ford's hands tighten on the steering wheel.

I shrug. "Hey, I might not change diapers, but I'm here for you. We'll get this figured out. First line of business is making sure it's yours."

Ford nods as though it sounds like a good plan, then he zooms into the parking garage of the condo building where his parents' penthouse is. "Thanks for coming. You know my dad won't go nearly as ballistic with you two here."

"You owe me big. Like, give me this car big," I say.

He parks in his designated spot and we all file out, Maksim stretching and limping.

"So tell us what happened with Saige?" Maksim asks.

"I'm not kissing and telling," I say as we head toward the elevator doors.

We can go right from the parking garage to the penthouse with Ford's special key card. The minute the elevator doors open into the foyer of his parents' penthouse, his dad's voice can be heard.

As though he heard the ding of the elevator over his yelling, Ford's dad walks out into the foyer, his slippers clicking on the marble floor. "Oh look, it's the three musketeers." He throws up his hands.

Ford's mom comes around the corner and smiles at us. "Boys. Come in." She hugs Maksim and me, ignoring Ford.

"No hug, Mom?" Ford says.

She turns and smacks him on the back of the head. "How's that for a hug? I lecture you and lecture you about safe sex. And what good did that do? You get some girl pregnant."

Ford scowls. "Jesus. I always use condoms."

"Well, I also tell you to keep it in your pants, but you don't listen." She focuses back on us. "Want something to eat, boys? Great game tonight."

"I'm fine," I say at the same time Maksim says, "What do you have?"

It's the fucking Jacobs. They have anything you want, and if not, they'll send someone out to get it, even in the middle of the night.

"Aiden." Mr. Jacobs nods as we pass. "Maksim."

"Hi, Mr. Jacobs," we mumble like high school kids who just got caught smoking pot.

"In my office, Ford. Now!"

Maksim and I scurry away. I'm not even sure why we're here. I think this time Mr. Jacobs won't hide his true feelings.

Following Mrs. Jacobs into the kitchen, I see that the chef's been awoken to feed us. What a life. I can't even imagine.

"Anything you want, boys," Mrs. Jacobs says.

"Boys." Imogen, Ford's younger sister, comes in and sits on a stool at the breakfast bar. Her pajamas are way too short and revealing, so I look away.

"Congrats, auntie," Maksim says over his bite of sandwich, holding it up to the chef in an appreciative gesture.

She rolls her eyes. "Oh please, do you really think it's his?"

This is the problem. What I said to Saige before I left isn't wrong. I've never been through it, but I've heard stories, seen careers ruined by someone saying it's their baby. On the flip side, I've seen plenty of athletes shuck their responsibilities and not take care of their children. But I know Ford will take care of the baby if it's his.

"Only a paternity test will tell us for certain," Mrs. Jacobs says.

Imogen rounds the corner of the large island and grabs an orange juice out of the fridge. "Helluva game tonight, Shamrock."

"Hey, what about me?" Maksim says. "Without me blocking, he'd never have gotten that point in the second period." He turns to the chef. "Do you have any chips?"

"Did you not eat dinner?" I ask him.

"I did, but I'm a growing boy." He pats his flat stomach.

Imogen laughs.

The elevator dings again, and a minute later, we hear Ford yell, "What the hell is *she* doing here?"

"I think Lena just arrived." Imogen holds up her finger.

We all laugh. Lena is the Jacobs' family PR rep, but pretty much her sole responsibility is Ford because he's always "fucking up," as Mr. Jacobs puts it.

I pull out my phone. "I gotta make a phone call."

"Who to?" Imogen asks.

"Drake's got a girlfriend," Maksim says with a chuckle.

I crinkle my nose. "Yeah, she wears my letterman jacket and everything." I shake my head at Maksim.

"I thought she wore Joran's," Maksim hammers back— fuck, how did I forget about Joran?

Shit. Shit. Shit.

"Forgot about him, didn't you?"

"I'll be back."

I walk into the Jacobs' formal living room, which, if I

had to describe it, I would say looks like an antique store. With a grand piano. Always the grand piano in places like this. I don't even think any of the Jacobses play piano.

I decide that I don't want to wake Saige, so I opt for a quick text to tell her where I am and that I'll hopefully return to the room soon. Mr. Jacobs' yelling and Ford's talking back make me feel as though maybe I'm lying.

As I'm about to rejoin them in the kitchen, Mrs. Jacobs walks into the room. She's in her pajamas and she sits on the couch, looking over a dark Central Park and the New York skyline.

"I'm going to be a grandmother," she says. "I never dreamed it would happen at this age, but I suppose you boys are getting older now."

I sit down in a chair. "This girl could be lying, or it could be someone else's."

She shakes her head and rests her hand on her stomach. "I've always trusted my gut, and my gut tells me this is it. Something had to happen before those two would rip each other's heads off." She nods toward the hallway that leads to the office where we can still hear Ford and his dad going at each other.

"How will a baby improve that?"

She smiles. "Because a baby bonds people. Doesn't always keep them together, but it bonds them. Mr. Jacobs might seem harsh, but once he lays his eyes on his grandchild, their happiness will supersede all else."

"Still, I'm not sure you should get your hopes up."

"Oh, Aiden." She leans forward and pats my leg. "Sometimes the best things happen as a result of the worst things you could imagine."

I don't know why the next words leave my mouth except that I need to talk to someone because I fucked up.

But I don't want to look at anything between Saige and me as a fuckup. "Can I ask you a question?"

"Always."

"I've been falling for this woman, but she's seeing my agent. I don't think it's serious between them or anything, but I slept with her tonight." I throw my head back because all I saw was her and I forgot about Joran. I'm a total douchebag.

She pats my leg again. "You boys… the first question you need to answer is how much she means to you."

"A lot. I haven't felt this way—ever."

"Then you challenge him to a duel." She chuckles.

"A duel?"

"You fight for her. Your story is as old as time. Two men falling for the same woman. If she means that much to you and you honestly believe you're the better one for her, then you need to fight for her. And just to clarify, I'm not talking about fists."

I chuckle now. "I know."

"Well, forgive me, but you know my son."

I laugh and stand, knowing what I need to do. "I gotta go." I kiss her cheek. "Thank you for the advice."

"Any time, son, and please help Ford through this. He's capable, but he's going to believe he isn't. Show him he is for me."

"Definitely."

I go into the kitchen to tell Maksim I'm leaving, and I say goodbye to Imogen.

Once I'm in a taxi, I text the first person I need to make it right with.

Me: *Are you home or traveling?*

Three dots appear just as I figured they would. He's never without his phone.

Joran: *Home. What happened? Is there something I need to know?*

Me: *No, just curious. I'll talk to you in the morning.*

Joran: *You sure?*

Me: *Positive.*

My next stop is the airport.

---

*T*figure seven o'clock in the morning is a respectable time to knock on Joran's door. He's probably been up for hours anyway.

He opens the door wearing silk boxers. "Okay, now I'm freaking out. What the hell is going on?" He ushers me in as though the police are looking for me and I'm a criminal.

"We need to talk."

We walk through the kitchen toward the back patio by the pool and something in red catches my eye. A brunette in skimpy red lingerie is pulling apart an orange at the kitchen table.

"Viola, say hello to Aiden. Aiden, this is Viola."

I stop in my tracks and tilt my head, making sure I understand the situation. "New roommate?"

Joran laughs. "Sure, man, come on." He slaps me on the back to go outside.

Once we're away from Viola, I don't take a seat like Joran does. "Who is she really?"

"Have you been out of the game that long? Why do you think she's here?"

"I think you're fucking her."

"Give the man a prize." He claps. "Now sit your ass down."

"You son of a bitch. How could you?" Before I can think better of it, I punch him in the mouth.

He holds his bloody lip, eyeing me. "Why the hell would you do that?" He stands. "Do you know her? Is she someone else's?"

I point inside the house. "I don't know who she is, and it doesn't matter. What about Saige? You're fucking around on her."

He grabs a napkin and heads inside before coming back with some ice. I pace in front of the pool, my fists clenching at my sides.

"You're gonna have to start from the beginning," Joran says.

"You and Saige and now you and Viola. Did you tell Saige? Or are you just fucking around behind her back like always?"

He shakes his head. "Aiden, I'm not with Saige."

I still and look at him.

He tries to hold both his hands in the air, but one hand is still holding his ice pack. "I'm not. I swear."

"But she said…"

"She broke it off with me weeks ago. We're very different people who want different things. I don't have time for a girlfriend, and frankly, I don't think she even wanted to be my girlfriend anyway."

I crouch down and bury my head in my hands. "She lied?"

"I'm completely lost. Is this why you're here so early?

Because you thought I was messing around on her?" Joran sits down and holds the ice to his lip.

I blow out a breath. "I'm here to win her from you."

He laughs. "And you thought I was going to fight you for her? Hell, you know whatever is mine is yours."

I wince at his words. "I like her, Joran. But to be honest, I'm not sure she feels the same way. She's been telling me you were together this entire time."

Though when I think back on it, I guess she didn't outright say that. Though she didn't dissuade me from thinking it either.

He leans back in his chair. "I don't know what to tell you, Aid, but don't do too much damage when she's in charge of your superstition. We have a few more weeks before trade deadlines. You need her until then at least."

I wave him off. "I'm out. I'll call you later."

I leave Joran and sit on the stairs outside his house before calling an Uber. Saige lied to me. Why? I can't think of one reason why she would unless she wanted to play games with me. Regardless, I'm getting to the bottom of it.

CHAPTER 22

"I do like the idea of stripping your clothes off."

Saige

’m at my desk, pissed off. I haven’t heard from Aiden at all, and he had some random guy from the team come and pick up his bag, saying it would travel back with them on the plane. No mention of where Aiden was, and he hasn’t returned a call or a text I’ve sent him.

“Tweetie says he wasn’t on the plane,” Tedi says, trying to make me feel better.

“I don’t really care where he was.”

I was all ready to tell him about Joran and explain why I kept the truth to myself for weeks. I wanted to tell him how scared I was, but then when we were together last night, it all felt so right and made my fear dissipate.

“We’re having a girls’ night tonight. Raunchy reality television, ice cream, and wine.”

“Not white,” I say.

“Only red. White is dead to me now.” Tedi pushes back from her desk and she’s about to stand when the office door opens. “Out!”

Aiden stands there. “Tedi, where is she?”

“Not here for douchebags like you.” She jumps up when he doesn’t leave and tries to stand between him and me, raising her small fists as though she’d punch him.

“You’re kidding me, right?” He stares down at her.

Pulling cash out of his pocket, he throws some on her desk. "Go buy yourself some shoes or something."

"That's so insulting. Why do you assume I want shoes? Maybe I want to go buy a new scope for my gun, huh?" She puts her head right in front of his, standing on her tiptoes. She's truly the best friend a girl can have.

"Buy whatever you want. I need to talk to Saige alone."

Tedi stops and turns around, looking at me. I nod. "You're lucky I didn't go all apeshit on you."

Aiden chuckles skeptically.

"I told Tweetie to slam you into the boards." She picks up her purse and the cash he left on her desk.

"He's my teammate. That's not how it works. Unless he messed around with Saige, I wouldn't touch him." His eyes lock with mine as he says it, and I ignore the swooning feeling in my stomach.

I need to remember that he left me high and dry after having sex with me.

"I'll just take my lunch early," Tedi says to me.

I wave her off and don't bother standing from my desk. Once the door shuts, Aiden locks it before stomping over to me.

"Have a seat, Mr. Drake." I motion to the chair on the other side of the desk.

Apparently he prefers to stand with his arms crossed as though he has some reason to be pissed at me. "I'm fine like this."

"Suit yourself. Are you here to talk about your social media? Everything seems good on that front even though you left the girl you fucked in a hotel room and now she's pissed off." Okay, so my whole indifferent act didn't last.

"First of all, I didn't fuck some girl in a hotel room. I slept with *you*. The one woman who's been driving me crazy since I met her. The one woman who kept giving me the hand and saying she was dating someone else. But come to find out, that was all a lie."

I straighten in my chair. "What are you talking about?"

"I went to Joran's to apologize for sleeping with you and tell him I wanted a chance with you and that I felt I was the better man for you. Imagine my surprise when he had another woman there. How do you think I reacted, Saige?" He slides his hands into his pockets and rocks back on his heels. "For me to think he was cheating on you... what do you think I did to my agent of ten years? The guy who's had my back over and over again."

I close one eye and wince. "Did you hit him?"

"Hell yeah, I did."

Okay, do not swoon over that. Remember what it was like in that hotel room when that strange man came to ask for his bag and made you feel like a random hookup.

"I'm sorry," I say.

"Sorry? Why did you lie to me all these weeks? Is this some type of game to you?"

I sigh and stand, looking out the window even though there's only a view of the parking lot. At least if I don't look at Aiden, I won't chicken out of this. "I felt as though if you thought I was still dating him, it would keep us from crossing lines. I thought it would be enough. But I was wrong." I let my head fall forward.

"Do you not want to be with me?" The anger is gone from his voice, but it's replaced with insecurity. I've never heard that tone in Aiden's voice before.

"I'm scared. So scared," I admit, tears pricking my eyes. "I've been here before and I wasn't enough. Who's to say I'm enough now?"

His hands land on the glass above my head and he cages me against the window. "You're all I think about. It's been torture having to be with you but not being able to touch you. I'm not the man who hurt you in the past." He runs his cheek along mine. "You're the girl for me."

"Maybe it was just lust and now that you've slept with me—"

"Then why am I here now?" His mouth dips to my neck, kissing me. "I'm not going to hurt you, Saige."

I swivel around and stare at him. Genuine care looks back at me. I run my hands down the stubble just starting on his cheeks, then up through his hair. "Promise you won't break me?"

"Promise," he says softly. "As long as you don't break me."

I insert my finger into the waistband of his jeans and tug him toward me. "I'm sorry for lying."

"I'm sorry for leaving you at the hotel. I thought I was doing the right thing by handling Joran so you wouldn't have to. Then after I found out the truth, I just… needed a minute."

"I have a question." He steps forward and I unbutton his jeans. We both watch my hands. "Am I your first relationship?"

"Sadly, yes."

"Rule number one—a text can do wonders. Just a text to say what you're doing and to no longer expect you, and I won't get mad."

He nods. "Texting is my friend. Got it."

"Rule number two…"

"Should I get a notepad?"

"No." I laugh, and my two fingers take hold of his zipper. "We do things together. I'm not a damsel in distress. We're a team."

"Okay."

"Rule number three…"

He inhales a deep breath. "What?"

"You can fuck me whenever you want now."

I look up and his eyes smolder with unbridled need.

"That's my favorite rule." His hands fall to my hips. "And can I just say, I like the skirts." He pulls the fabric up, circling us around so I'm at the edge of my desk.

"I'll have to remember that."

I push his jeans and boxer briefs down to his ankles, and he tugs my skirt up to my waist and pushes my thong aside, his finger running the length of my folds. "Soaked."

I nod and grab a hold of him. "Hard."

We laugh, until he bends me back and puts the tip of his dick right at my entrance. "I swear tonight you'll get slow and loving, but after all the drama, I need you something fierce right now."

"Me too. Take me however you want."

He thrusts into me. "Fuck, you're a perfect fit."

I grab the edge of my desk to anchor myself so he can thrust in and out of me. "Aiden."

His finger goes to my clit and he circles it, stirring a hunger inside me I want to savor, but my orgasm is barreling to the forefront like a raging animal and I can't control it. I shatter under his hand and he continues to glide in and out, all the way to the hilt, until he grunts and collapses on top of me.

I'm a trembling mess on my desk when he straightens, grabbing a few Kleenex to clean up the mess. After we're both clean, he takes me in his arms, sitting in my office chair.

"Thank you."

"For what?" I say, listening to his heartbeat start to return to normal.

"For trusting me."

"The same could be said for you."

He looks at me, obviously not understanding.

"Frankie told me about your niece."

"She did?" He turns his face away from me, but I nudge him with my hand to look at me.

"She did, and we don't have to do any social media if you don't want to. You could've told me."

He puts his finger to my lips. "It's fine. You've done nothing but be professional on there. Although I will post a picture of the two of us at some point."

I shake my head. "You will not."

He tightens his arms around my waist. "You don't understand. I want the whole entire world to know you're mine. Look, I punched my agent, who's had my back for years. Can you imagine what I'd do to a stranger if he hit on you? It's for the public's best interests really."

I laugh and stand, sliding my skirt down over my ass.

"Ditch and come home with me. We can have a bonfire and sex on the beach," he says.

That does sound nice. "I should work."

"Come on. I have a game tomorrow night and I want at least one full night with you in my bed." He rests his chin on my stomach.

I stare down at him, my fingers moving through his silky strands of dark hair. "Okay. But this cannot happen all the time. I do have work."

He stands and towers over me. Picking up discarded clothes, he puts them back on. "Let's go. Are you gonna tell Tedi she can come back?"

I straighten my desk because Tedi will never let me live it down if she knows I had sex on my desk. "She'll come back on her own. You were really angry when you showed up here, huh?"

"I could say the same about you. It turned me on." His dark eyes sparkle.

"So we're in agreement that make-up sex is awesome then."

"Not enough to start a fight over, but I do like the idea of stripping your clothes off." He grins at me.

We leave my office and head down to his SUV. After a quick trip to my place, he drives us to his house that overlooks the gulf. This is something I could definitely get used to.

CHAPTER 23

"You're playing games."

Saige

If someone had asked me where Aiden Drake, center for the Florida Fury, lived, I never would've guessed here. The house isn't huge by any standard, but it's on the beach with its own pool and hot tub in the back. He has neighbors, but none of them are too close, allowing him enough privacy to do as he pleases.

"Go ahead outside, I'll get us some drinks," he says.

I walk through the house to the sliding glass doors and the patio that overlooks the Gulf of Mexico. It's a beautiful sight. I imagine myself enjoying the sound of waves crashing on the sand when I wake up in the morning.

"What do you think?" he asks, stepping outside with a beer for him and a glass of wine for me.

"It's beautiful." I accept the glass and he stands next to me, staring at what I assume is his stretch of private beach.

"Took me forever to find. I saved for my first two years in the league, living with Maksim. I was close to buying land and building until this popped up on the market. I've had to do a lot of renovations, but I can't beat the seclusion. And the view." He tips back his beer.

"I agree. Have you always played for the Florida Fury?"

"Yep. They drafted me and I've been here ever since.

Another reason I don't really want to go anywhere else. I've made my life here. I mean, look at this. What if I end up in some high-rise in New York? I know I'd hate it."

I walk around the pool and sit on his lounge furniture. "Well, you wouldn't have to give this up, but your seasons are pretty long."

He nods. "I'm still holding out hope Gerhardt doesn't trade me. He's been off my ass since I started playing well, so hopefully it continues that way."

"Less than three weeks." I hold out my wine glass and he clinks his bottle against it.

"I really don't wanna talk hockey with you," he says, sliding closer to me on the sofa.

"What do you want to talk about?"

"I don't wanna talk. I wanna make out like a couple of teenagers." He nuzzles his head into the crook of my neck, kissing and licking his way up until he reaches my mouth. When his tongue plunges inside, I almost drop my wine glass—he's that good of a kisser.

When he closes the kiss, I say, "You could show me the rest of the place."

He sets his beer on the table and takes my wine glass, putting it next to it. "Deal."

Picking me up and lifting me over his shoulder, Aiden carries me into his house, up a flight of stairs, and down a hall to a master bedroom most people would give their firstborn to have.

He drops me on the bed, and I soak it all in. It's decorated very minimalistic with a wooden-frame king bed and white bedding. It's the view that makes the room what it is, and the floor-to-ceiling sliding windows that look out over the gulf has my jaw on the floor.

"Tell me what it's like to watch a storm coming in from here. It must be amazing." I imagine a lazy morning in

Aiden's arms, hearing the thunder roll in and watching it from bed while we make love over and over.

"You'll find out one of these days. Promise."

I hope so, because for a minute there on the drive over here, I wasn't so sure this is reality and not some dream I've conjured up.

He opens all the windows, letting in the ocean smell and sounds.

"Can I move in?" I ask without thinking it through.

"That's better than me kidnapping you."

I laugh and he walks over, stepping into my open legs, tilting my head back and running his thumb over my bottom lip. "I'm so happy you're here with me."

I hold on to his wrist, looking into his mesmerizing eyes. "Me too."

"When I thought you were playing games, I had no idea what I was gonna do because I knew I'd never get you out of my head. You've captivated me since the first time I met you."

It does seem crazy when you think about it that only last month we were walking Mr. Gerhardt's property during that New Year's Eve party.

"You can have all the midnight kisses you want," I say.

He dips his thumb into my mouth and I lightly nibble on it while running my tongue around it. He groans and watches me intently. My fingers unbutton his pants and tug them down over his hips until they fall to his ankles. He steps out of them and I palm his hard length, loving that I have this effect on him. That I'm the one who turned this man on so much.

"Step back," I say, and he does as I ask. "The first time I saw your cock in the locker room, I about died."

"Too big. I get that a lot." He laughs as if it's a joke, but he shouldn't be.

"It took every ounce of willpower not to jump you."

"I wouldn't have complained."

I fall to my knees in front of him and pull the front of his boxer briefs down under his balls. His breath hitches as he watches me intently. I've never been this turned on before, but the look in his eyes as I watch him anticipating me taking him into my mouth is my undoing.

"You're gorgeous." He runs the backs of his knuckles down the side of my face. I'm starting to love the fact he's not shy in telling me what he thinks at every moment.

I wrap my hand around his base, twisting my hand up to his tip. His hand snakes around to the nape of my neck and I lean forward, my tongue swirling around his tip, tasting the bead of precum. The groan that erupts from his throat undoes me, and I swallow down his length and pull him back out.

The tightening of his fingers in my hair tells me he likes it, so I do it again and am rewarded with the sting of my scalp from him tugging my hair. From that moment, I follow his nonverbal cues. I want to find out what he likes because suddenly, pleasing this man in the bedroom has become a quest I can conquer.

His hips push forward, so I take him as deep as I can, choking, and his growl bounces off the wall. I hope no one is walking by on the beach.

"Fuck, it should be illegal that you're so good at this."

I almost laugh but contain myself until he's circling his hips, swearing and praising me all at once.

"I'm coming," he warns seconds before he bursts into my mouth, the salty taste of him sliding down my throat. "Fuck, you've ruined me."

I laugh, falling back on my heels and licking my lips clean. "I'll take the compliment."

He urges me up until he can lift me and toss me on the bed. "Payback time."

His show of brute strength only makes me wetter. I slide up to the top of the bed, more than eager to have his mouth on me again.

"First we need to get you naked."

I undo my blouse while he works on my skirt.

After we're done, he stands at the foot of the bed, staring at me. "Do you have any idea how many times I've visualized you right here, in my bed, naked and waiting for me to pleasure you?"

I shake my head.

His fingers run over my ankles gently. "Tell me you've wanted me as much as I've wanted you."

"Aiden, I've wanted you inside me since New Year's Eve. Every day being near you but not able to tell you I wanted you was excruciating."

He grins. "That's what I wanna hear."

"It's why I couldn't always watch you skate. It turns me on so much, and knowing I might never get to experience this..."

He tugs me down the bed by my ankles and goes to his knees in front of my center. "Experience what exactly?"

"You."

"Be more specific, Saige." His tone is dangerously erotic, and my core tightens when I look into his dark eyes.

"Having you inside me."

"My tongue or my cock?"

Oh god, he's going to dirty-talk me now.

"Both."

His fingers lightly explore my inner thighs, teasing me with a barely-there touch to my pussy. "Which do you prefer?"

"Your cock."

He situates himself between my legs. "So you don't want to feel my tongue on you?" He blows lightly on my core and my hips rise off the bed. "Want to change your answer?"

I shake my head.

"Okay then. You don't want me to continue doing this?" Using his tongue, he circles my clit then sucks it into his mouth.

My hips burst from the bed and he laughs against me.

"You're playing games," I pant.

He comes out from between my legs and looks at me. "Damn right I'm playing games. Don't worry though, I'm not sure which I like more either. Licking your pussy or having my cock buried deep inside you."

"Why must we choose?" I say with a smile.

"Smart girl." He puts my legs on his shoulders, and before long, I'm writhing underneath him, begging him for more. More of anything he has to offer.

Please don't let me wake up alone again to find out this was all a dream.

CHAPTER 24

Aiden

The best part of owning a private beach is that at night, when most people are in bed, I can build a bonfire and have a naked Saige in my arms with only a blanket covering us.

"I have s'mores stuff," I offer.

We opted to order in dinner because I didn't want to cook and waste any moment I could have my hands on her. We've finally gotten to a place where I don't have to hide my feelings—somewhere I've wanted to be for weeks as I've gotten to know her—and I want to relish every moment.

"Hmm… maybe in a bit. What ended up happening with Ford?" she asks, leaning her head on my shoulder.

"Last I heard, they were arranging a paternity test and waiting on the results."

She turns to look at me and the moonlight on her face makes her even more beautiful. "Is that something you've ever had to worry about?"

"Getting a woman pregnant?" If she thinks she's being sly, she's wrong. "Is this your way of asking me how many women I've been with?"

She sighs. "Well, you are Aiden Drake. I didn't mean to outright ask you, but you hear the story so often."

I tighten my arms around her. "My whole life has been hockey. Sure, I've had random hookups, I can't deny that, but that's all they've been. And I've always worn protection."

"And Ford doesn't?" she asks.

I really don't want to spend the night talking about my best friend's sex life. "Ford is complicated. I know the way he comes off, but he's a really good guy. He'd have my back no matter what. One day I know he'll figure his shit out and be the guy I know he can be."

"You're a good friend." Her fingers run along the length of mine.

"Why do you say that?"

"Because you left me naked in bed to make sure he was all right. I could've run, you know?"

I slide my face down her neck and kiss her like crazy. "Is that so? You were gonna run from me? Good thing I'm faster than you."

She giggles, and I capture her lips in a searing kiss that makes me feel like it will never be enough. The feelings I'm developing for Saige are scary if I think too hard about them, but when I'm around her, all I want is for her to never leave my side.

"I want to be caught anyway." She kisses me one more time.

We watch the flames from the bonfire for a while, a comfortable silence falling over us.

"Come home with me," I say.

She turns around, her forehead wrinkled. "What? I'm at your home now."

"My childhood home. We fly to Chicago next week. After the game, I'm heading home to see my family."

"What? But—"

"I know it's soon, but you were coming to Chicago

anyway and I'd love for you to meet them. They rarely get out here, and other than in the off-season, I only see them once or twice a year."

"Meet the parents?"

"Don't worry, Phil and Barb are nice midwestern folk."

She stares into the fire. "I worry we're moving too fast. Like you're going to wake up and be sick of me. Regret what we have or feel trapped."

I hate that she has these negative thoughts, thanks to that dipshit Jeremy. I'd like to kick his ass for making her think she has to worry about shit like this.

"Not gonna happen."

She turns around and gets on her knees, the blanket falling off her, leaving her skin glowing with the reflection of the flames. "You chased me, Aiden. What if that's all this was?"

I push a piece of her hair away from her face. "Is that why you've been running? Because you thought I was all about the chase?"

"No. I just didn't want to get hurt, but listen, it happens all the time. Once you get what you wanted, it doesn't have the same appeal as it once did."

I pull her down to me and situate her so we're lying on the blanket, pulling the other one over her in case anyone walks by. "I chased an NHL career my entire life, and guess what happened after I got drafted?"

"What?"

"I fucking loved it and I still do until this day. Sure, being in the slump sucked, but I still loved playing."

"That's different. There's no substitution or competition for that. There isn't some other hockey league at the same level that's going to steal your attention away."

I place my finger next to her chin and nudge her to look at me. "My attention will always be on you." I take her hand and place it over my heart. "Feel this? That's what you do to me. Nothing is going to change. I wasn't in it for the chase, Saige. I was in it for the win."

She bites her bottom lip. "Promise?"

I kiss her briefly and hover my lips over hers. "Promise."

She snakes her hand around my neck and drags me down to her. Before either of us can come up for air, I'm sliding over her, between her legs, and pushing inside her. I'll spend a lifetime convincing her she's the one for me if that's what it takes.

---

*S*aige is still at my house the next day when I have to get to the game for warmups and a team meeting. We went back to her office this morning to get her car, then swung by her place to grab some other things for her to spend the night again.

I set the glass of white wine on the bathroom counter. "Don't you want to sit with the wives and girlfriends?" I ask, wanting her to be there and get to know everyone.

She shakes her head. "We've been over this. You need to remain single on social media. Believe me, people are scoping that area for anyone new."

I wrap my arms around her from behind and look at her in the mirror. "I want the whole world to know you're mine."

"We know and that's enough." She pats my hands. "Remember, you put me in charge of your social media and I'm telling you what's best."

"But—"

She swivels around in my arms. God, I love her naked.

No better sight in the world. "But nothing. This is what's best."

I blow out a breath and leave her to turn on the shower. Might as well get ready for my game. She is the professional in this area, but I can't help but feel annoyed that I have to live according to what a bunch of strangers might think.

"Now, Mr. Drake." She picks up the wine glass. "Why don't you get in the shower?"

I step in and admire her walking toward me. Even after how much sex we've had over the past twenty-four hours, my dick still salutes her. "This is the best sight of you throwing wine at my face yet."

She tosses the wine at me and steps inside the stall, kissing me.

"Thanks," I whisper, and she licks the side of my face.

"You do know this doesn't help your game, right?" she murmurs against my skin.

I playfully smack her ass. "Shame on you. First rule of being a hockey player's girlfriend is that you buy into all the superstitions they do."

"If you say so, my lucky number thirteen." She pats my cheek and steps out, but I pull her into the shower with me and she squeals.

"Lucky is the keyword," I say before shutting the shower door and pressing her back to the tile.

---

*A*n hour later, I'm dressed in my suit and she's still lying around in a robe, tempting me to stay.

"So after the game, we're ditching and coming back here," I remind her.

Tedi and Tweetie have already initiated some sort of get-together that I said no to while Saige said maybe.

"I don't want to leave Tedi alone."

I blow out a breath. That means we'll all be getting together after the game. "I want to celebrate." She opens her mouth. "With you and only you."

She giggles. "You've had me all day and all night."

"Yes, and it's not enough. I'm insatiable when it comes to you." I wrap her in my arms.

"We'll talk after the game."

"Fine." I kiss her, my body fighting with my brain for me to stay. "See you at the game. If I win, will you do a striptease tonight?"

"If you lose, I'll do a striptease. If you win, you can tie me up."

I groan. "Fuck, Saige, now I'm hard again."

Her hand goes between my legs and massages my half chub, quickly shifting it into raging hard-on mode. "I like you hard."

"I'd like not to play hockey with a hard dick."

"So flashing you while you play is off-limits?"

I kiss her one last time, still not ready to let her go. "I'd say you could flash me if you wouldn't be showing millions of others your tits that are now half mine."

"Half?"

"I figure everything is fifty-fifty. My dick is half yours." I shrug.

"That's an interesting way of thinking about it," she says, cocking one eyebrow, palming me still. "Because I think of your dick as mine and only mine."

"Fair enough, so your tits and pussy are mine then." I slide my hand inside her robe and cup her wet pussy. "And I need to get out of here before that robe comes off and I fuck you over the back of the couch."

"No objections here," she says.

I bring my fist to my mouth and bite down—hard. "You're gonna make my dick fall off." I backstep to the door, watching her every move.

"One last thing to remember me by," she says and unhooks her robe, letting it fall to the floor.

"Tell me we'll come home after the game tonight and I'll play the best game ever," I say.

She pauses then smiles. "Fine, we'll come home after."

"Every goal is for you!" I wink and turn around before I don't have the willpower to leave.

As I climb into my SUV, that old feeling is back in my chest. The lucky one I always used to feel on the way to my games. That was, until my game went to shit. I used to thrive off that feeling and I know I have only one person to thank for its return—Saige Fowler, my girlfriend.

CHAPTER 25

"I forgot we were in public. Let's get you out of here."

Saige

$\mathcal{I}$ fly into Chicago and I shouldn't be surprised when I find Aiden waiting in my hotel room. Tweetie wanted Tedi in attendance at this game, so we flew in together, but she has her own room. Man, has that relationship transformed from a fuck-it bucket list item to something more, but Tedi still won't admit it.

"What are you doing here?" I ask with a grin.

Aiden holds out his arms. I leave my suitcase by the door and go over to the king-size bed, crawling up into the shelter of his arms.

"We have to do the honorary tour of the town. Especially now that we're a couple."

One of the things I love about Aiden is that he isn't afraid to say we're a couple. I've still been fighting him tooth and nail about posting a picture of us together on social media, but I'm flattered that he wants to shout it from the rooftops. I've seen the backlash too many times to allow him to do it though.

"What did you have in mind?" I ask.

"Since it's colder than hell out there, how about the planetarium?"

"Perfect. Let me just change from my airplane clothes."

"I'm sure you need help getting undressed. Allow me."

His hand slides down the front of me and he undoes the button on my jeans, his hand gliding down past the lace top of my panties.

"I'm not even going to argue." I lean back and kiss his neck.

———

*B*y the time we're finished, we both take showers and get dressed to head out, we don't have a ton of time to explore Chicago.

"Who won the card game on the plane?" I ask.

He laughs. "I did. Told you, it's like all my luck is back the way it was before."

Aiden's been talking like that for a week. He says that ever since we got together, he's had that old feeling inside him that his lucky streak is back. It worries me, but I'm trying to remain positive. I mean, who would've thought me throwing wine at his face would get him to perform so well after he'd hit a real slump? I guess it's better to be optimistic rather than pessimistic.

He secures his baseball hat low over his eyes and we leave the hotel in a cab headed toward the planetarium. We're lucky since it's a weekday and other than some buses from school field trips, there aren't a bunch of guests here. Aiden pays and we walk in, hand in hand.

"Come on, let's go somewhere dark."

"Has anyone ever told you you're a nympho?" I ask and he laughs.

"That's not an insult if you were hoping it was."

"I merely meant that you can't keep your hands to yourself."

He removes his hands from me and holds them in the air. "Fine, no more touching for the rest of the day."

I shake my head at him. "There's no way you can keep up with that."

He stops us off to the side and some school kids walk by. "Let's make a bet."

"Nothing sexual," I say.

"So no to anal then?" he says with a dead serious face.

"Oh my god." I look around to see if anyone heard him, but no one is paying us any attention. "What else you got?"

He thinks for a moment. I can tell the minute the idea hits his brain because he smiles. "A picture on social media."

My smile falters and I'm pretty sure I'm giving him a death glare. I might be the only girl dating a professional hockey player who doesn't want everyone to know.

"Fine. I'm only taking this bet because you're going to lose, Drake." I poke him in the chest. He's about to clasp my finger and my eyebrows rise.

"Are you saying no touching at all?"

I sigh. "Hand-holding and a hand on the small of the back. That's it."

"I'm good with that." He links our hands together and walks us toward the planetarium portion of the museum. It'll be dark in there and he shouldn't be recognized. I know it will drive him crazy not to be able to touch me in here too. "What do you get if I lose and touch you? I mean, other than the pleasure of my hands on you."

I laugh and playfully push him. "You listen to me and stay quiet about us for as long as I say."

"Deal." He puts out his hand and I'm about to slide my hand in, but he raises it and lifts his hat for a second. "You thought you had me."

I laugh. "I did not."

We go into the planetarium. He picks the last row, which will be good for him not to be recognized.

After learning about stars and planets, I'm starved. Honestly, I loved hearing all the interesting facts about our solar system. And Aiden was good, not touching me once, even to hold my hand.

We're just leaving the planetarium when a kid screams, "*Aiden Drake!*"

We both turn, and one of the kids from a field trip has his finger pointed right at Aiden. He turns to me and has to decide what to do in a split second. Deny the kid and say he's wrong, or admit it's him and be bombarded. Since he has to be at warmups soon, we don't have a ton of time.

"Sorry," he says to me and walks over to the kid.

Soon all the kids are circled around, and I watch from the sidelines, far enough away so no one will pay me any attention. But I do pull out my phone and snap a few pictures to put on his Instagram account.

Aiden's patient, even when a teacher offers him a Sharpie so he can sign everything from brown paper lunch bags to the shirts the kids are wearing. The boys and girls ask him questions as though he's a visitor in their class.

"That goal you scored the other night was amazing. How do you do that?" one boy asks.

Aiden glances back to check on me, and I wave for him to continue. I'm fine. Watching him with the kids stirs a feeling inside my stomach I can't explain. Before meeting Aiden, I didn't know much about hockey. At least not hockey players. Doing research after I took Aiden on as a client, I found out a few things about Aiden. He was rarely ever photographed outside practices, games, and any official team duties like meeting with fans or charitable efforts. He was known to keep his head down and play the game without a lot of drama off the ice. There's also talk about him being one of the best centers the game has ever seen and will more than likely hit the Hall of Fame at some point.

I think that's what spurred me to agree to the drink throwing. Someone deemed one of the best at his game shouldn't go down without a fight. And if he thought me throwing a drink was going to make a difference, well, might as well give it a shot.

"What superstitions do you have?" a little girl asks.

"Yeah, do you eat something special before a game?" a boy chimes in.

"Do you wear your socks for the entire season without washing them?" another kid blurts out.

"Gross!" A group of girls make faces as if that's the most disgusting thing they've ever heard.

Again, Aiden looks back at me before crouching and whispering to them. All the kids make a sound like they can't believe it, then their eyes are on me. I don't even want to know.

"Come on, kids, we need to get going. Thank Mr. Drake for being so nice and stopping to talk to us today."

"Thank you, Mr. Drake," the kids say in unison.

But before they leave, the teacher stops and Aiden jots down something on a piece of paper and hands it to her. She eyes him with appreciation and thanks him one more time.

Coming back over to me, Aiden gets stopped by a few people asking for selfies now that he's been outed. Once he's in the clear, he meets me, placing his hands on either side of the cement wall behind me.

"Careful, you're getting close there," I say.

"I'm not touching you," he whispers, his breath on my neck.

"That was sweet of you. What did the teacher want?"

"Jealous?"

"No." And I'm not jealous. Okay, slightly, but I'm not worried at all.

"She wondered if I'd be willing to come in and talk at the school. Maybe bring some other players."

"That's sweet."

"I should probably do more of that."

I shrug. "What did you tell those kids when they asked about your superstitions?"

He chuckles, his eyes never leaving mine. "I told them you're my lucky charm. That ever since I met you, I've been having some great games."

I shake my head. "No white wine?"

"Ah, they're little. Didn't want them stealing their mom's wine and throwing it in each other's faces."

I rest my palm on his cheek, unable to not be affectionate with him.

"Note that *you're* touching *me*."

"I know. I can't help it. You're amazing. You win the bet."

"What can I say? I'm quite the catch."

His tone is joking, and I wonder if he really doesn't realize how great of a catch he is. Any girl would be lucky to have him, and here I am, the lucky girl. I need to calm my overzealous brain and remember he chose me, end of story.

"Aiden," someone calls.

We both look, only to be surprised by the flash of a camera.

"Good luck tonight," the person says. They look like an average Joe, not a reporter or anything.

I ask quietly, "Do people really take your picture without asking?"

He nods. "Unfortunately, yes. Come on, I forgot we were in public. Let's get you out of here."

We head to a taxi and climb in to go have some of the deep-dish pizza Chicago is known for. The taxi driver asks where to and we tell him to take us to his favorite pizza place. Five minutes later, we're outside Lou Malnati's. An hour later, I have no idea how Aiden is going to skate if his stomach feels anything like mine.

"That was a lot," I say.

"Yeah, I'm gonna be slow on my skates tonight."

Once we get back to the hotel, Aiden's still able to do some pre-warmup workouts if you catch my drift. And I have to say—it didn't affect his performance at all.

CHAPTER 26

"Any woman willing to be with my
son gets points in my book."

Aiden

"*D*rake!" Coach Vittner yells from his temporary office in the Chicago locker room.

We won, so I have no idea why he sounds so pissed.

I walk in already dressed in my suit because my girl is waiting on me. "What's up, Coach?"

"Game schedule change. We've got our make-up game for when the wildfires canceled the one in California, so the team is flying out tomorrow morning for a game in two nights. I know you had plans to go to your parents', so I'm allowing you to fly in on game day since you've been on point lately. *But.*" He holds up his hands. "You better be there and ready to play. Do you understand?"

This puts a huge crimp in my plans. Saige and I were going to stay with my parents for a few days before she has to meet up with a basketball player in Milwaukee. With this change in plans, she'll have to miss my game in California. Fuck. I've obviously played without her there before —she didn't start coming until I gave her tickets—so I guess as long as we do the drink throwing before I leave, we should be good. It'll still be game day.

"What are you doing? Figuring out some Einstein equation? Did you hear me?" Coach says.

I nod. "Yes. Just thinking about the logistics, Coach. I'll

be there and ready."

"Good. Now in other news…" He walks by me and shuts the door. Either because Ford is singing again or because the celebration hasn't stopped. "Gerhardt called me into his office before we headed here."

"And?"

"We're a couple weeks shy of trade deadline. He didn't say anything about a trade, but the fact that you haven't seen the psychologist yet is a problem for him. Get your ass into her office. I've told him that you're harboring some sort of problems from your childhood, but that I'd work on you. You're one of the only two players left to see her."

"Who's the other?" I assume he'll say Ford, because he was adamant about it before.

"You and Petrov. Talk to him too. This isn't optional for you boys."

Ford went to see the psychologist? I'm shocked.

"As soon as we're back, I'll make my appointment." If what I need to do to stay on this team is have a counseling session, I'll do it.

"Take Petrov with you. Even if you have to drag him."

"Coach?" I laugh, and he shakes his head.

"I don't need any more problems on my roster. We're finally in a great position and if something happens and you get traded, I might as well call this season over. I'm old, Drake. I want the Cup."

I stand. "I'll do whatever it takes."

"See that you do. Have a good time with your family, but be ready to play. I see that blonde hanging around… don't let it detour you away from the big picture."

"It… she won't."

"Now leave. I need to call in Tweetie about his shitty penalty this evening."

I walk out of Coach's office and head back into the

locker room to grab my bags. Maksim is there at his locker, still undressing.

"Get your ass on that psychologist's couch," I tell him.

"Fuck that. I'm not doing that shit."

"We all have to. So far it's just you and me who haven't been. The captain and the assistant haven't seen her yet and we're supposed to represent for the team."

He turns around again in just his jockstrap. I don't get it. The man isn't shy in the least. "I'm not going."

"You will when I drag you."

Shit, maybe Coach is right and I will have to physically drag him.

"Have fun with your family and having them meet Saige. Don't worry about me." His blue eyes sparkle with mischief.

I point at him. "You're going."

"Don't eat too much cheese. It will bung you up and you won't be able to skate!" he calls and I flip him off, leaving the locker room.

*S*aige and I pack up and leave that night since we'll now have limited time with my family. We've decided to go stay at my parents' house.

"Did you call them to tell them we're coming?" she asks when we pull up in front of my parents' house and it looks like no one is home.

"They own a bar, so they're not even home yet." I glance at the time on the dash of our rental. "But they'll be here shortly. Gives you some time to get comfortable."

I park on the side of the driveway so my parents can pull into the garage. We grab our bags and I lead us into the house. It smells the same as it always does—the same candle my mom's been burning for years, vanilla and lilac —and it brings me back to my youth.

Our house is more country style than one would think after meeting my parents. And not that modern farmhouse decor, but pure country, like blue-and-white gingham, lace, doilies, and a lot of wood. Pictures of my sister and me from all ages line the stairway that creaks from the age of the house.

My parents don't have a ton of money, but they never let us go without anything either. And now that I do have money, they won't let me spend any of it on them.

"Come on, let's get our bags in the room."

"Will they be okay with us sleeping together?" She dodges the one deer my dad ever shot when he went hunting years ago. After that, he was only a fishing guy.

"We're adults. They'll be fine. One more flight." I open the door to reach my room that's actually the attic.

We climb the stairs and I see that nothing has changed. My full-size bed with a blue comforter still sits in the center of the space. Posters of hockey greats like Gretzky, Hull, Jagr, Lemieux, and Howe line the walls. Trophies and pucks with dates written on them fill the shelves my dad installed.

"So this is Aiden Drake's childhood bedroom, huh?" Saige sits on the bed and looks around. "Did you lose your virginity in here?"

"No." I stand by my small childhood desk. Seeing her on my bed is tempting, but my parents will be home soon and that's not exactly the first impression I want to give of Saige.

"I would've thought all the girls were hot for you."

I take a picture off the corkboard behind me and toss it to her on the bed. "This was me at sixteen." I was tall, lanky, wore braces, and had acne.

"You were cute."

I raise my eyebrows.

"I would've let you bring me up here." She leans back on her elbows and tilts her head as an invitation.

Oh, fuck it. I jump on the bed and she laughs as I climb over her. The bed squeaks like crazy and I realize this won't be good for tonight.

"Took you long enough." She giggles.

"I was respecting you."

"That ship sailed when you poured chocolate sauce on me and licked it off three nights ago."

I laugh and my lips find hers. Things between us don't stay PG for long because I'm grinding my hard-on into her core and she's moaning and tugging at my shirt to take it off. Maybe make-out sessions are out for us now.

Lights shine in my window and I draw the kiss to a close. "There's my parents."

She pushes me off her and I tumble to the floor since it's only a full-size bed.

"Oh jeez." She finger-combs her hair, pulling her shirt down.

Where'd the woman who was halfway to stripping me go?

I get up off the floor and hold out my hand. "Don't hold anything they say against me."

"That's scary and cryptic," she says with a smile.

I lead her down the two flights of stairs, and when we enter the kitchen, my parents are just coming in through the garage.

"Hey, Mom. Dad."

Although they knew I was coming, they weren't expecting me so soon and they both smile.

"Hey, Aid," my dad says and takes off his jacket.

"How are you, sweetie? Hell of a game tonight." Mom

hugs me. "Sorry for the smell. Bar life."

I forgot how much they smell when they get home.

My mom waits patiently, looking at Saige. Since my dad has yet to return from the bathroom, I figure I'll introduce them separately.

"Mom, this is Saige. Saige, this is the woman who raised me. Any problems, talk to her."

My mom laughs and swats at my arm. She holds out her hand. "Nice to meet you, Saige, and he's right, if he doesn't treat you right, I'm your first call. I'll put him in his place." She winks.

"Nice to meet you, and he's been nothing but a gentleman."

"I'm going to take a quick shower and get this gross smell off me. Are you guys hungry? I have pizzas in the freezer, or find whatever you want." My mom touches Saige's upper arm as she leaves the room. "Make yourself at home."

Saige smiles. I'm glad they seem to like one another, even if they have only spent a total of two minutes in the same room together.

"Are you hungry?" I ask. We didn't eat after the game and I'm starving, so I head to the freezer and pull out two pizzas.

"Maybe a little."

I preheat the oven and take the pizzas out of the plastic.

"Okay, better. I swear I can never take a shit in private." My dad comes out of the bathroom, looking down and adjusting his belt.

"Dad," I say quickly.

He looks up. "Whoops. Sorry. Hi, Saige, we've heard nothing about you but your name, but that's no surprise. Aiden could've been a monk. Thank goodness he's got a

hockey career because he wouldn't make it as a bartender."
My dad shakes Saige's hand.

"Hi, Mr. Drake," she says.

"Mr. Drake? My dad isn't here. It's Phil."

"Okay, Phil."

My dad takes notice of the frozen pizzas on the counter. "Pizza? I could've had them prepare you something at the bar."

"I should've stopped there on the way into town," I say.

"Great game tonight. Still so impressive. Can you believe this guy?" He puts his hand on my neck and squeezes. "Skating laps around me at only ten. I might not have been a pro, but I did play in high school."

"Dad was a goalie," I tell her.

"I knew when he was twelve and I couldn't block his shots anymore that this kid had something." He squeezes my neck again and my shoulders scrunch up.

No one could ever say my parents aren't proud of me. They've always been my biggest cheerleaders.

"Saige was a figure skater," I say.

My dad's hand leaves my neck, and he stares at her, looking impressed. "I have no idea how you people jump like that and expect to land on the ice."

Saige laughs. "They start you young when you have no fear."

"So what else? Where are you from?" My dad leans back against the counter.

"Don't you want to shower?" I ask my dad.

"Do you mind the smell of stale beer and cigarettes, Saige?"

"Like she'd say no," I say.

Saige smiles brightly. "I'm fine."

"Thank you." Dad sits at the table and pulls out the

paper. He's the only guy I know who reads the paper after midnight. "Your sister and everyone is coming over for brunch tomorrow."

I look at Saige. "We don't do breakfast because Mom and Dad sleep in."

"It's not sleeping in. It's our sleep schedule. If we were like everyone else our age, we'd be asleep for five hours by now and up with the roosters."

I smile. A year ago, I asked my parents if I could retire them or at least get help at the bar so they'd be able to live more normal lives. But they both declined, adamant that my money is my money. No matter how much I fought to tell them I'd never be where I was without them, they fought back that helping me is their job as parents. I'm not over the idea of retiring them though.

"Fair enough." The oven beeps and I place the frozen pizzas inside.

"Phil, get your lazy ass up and take a shower," my mom says upon her return. "Saige doesn't want to smell liquor and cigarettes the entire night, do you, sweetie?"

"She said it was fine," Dad argues back.

"What's she gonna say? She wants to please you."

"Please me?" Dad asks, already rising from the chair and putting down his reading glasses. "No worries there. Any woman willing to be with my son gets points in my book. He's hard to handle, am I right?"

Saige laughs and shakes her head. "He's great."

I catch my mom admiring the way Saige and I look at one another, so I go over and tuck my mother under my arm, kissing the top of her head.

"Go shower, Phil!" my mom yells.

"I was just admiring the scene. A little sappy, but it's cute." My dad winks at Saige and disappears upstairs.

I'll take sappy but cute. Beats lonely and alone any day.

Saige

The banging of a piano wakes me, and I grab my phone from the nightstand, seeing it's already nine in the morning.

I hit Aiden next to me. "It's nine!"

He lays his arm over my waist and pulls me closer to him. "And?"

"And someone is playing the piano. Not very well."

His eyes open, and he crawls out of bed. I've never seen him get out of bed this fast before. Pulling on a pair of sweats and a T-shirt, he nods for me to get up. "Ready to meet the bulldozer crew?"

"The who?" I ask, climbing out and putting on a pair of yoga pants and his Florida Fury sweatshirt. I fix my ponytail. "I feel like I need to get ready."

"Brunches in this family are casual at best. Showers are forbidden." He grabs my hand and leads me down the stairs.

The piano only gets louder with each flight of stairs we descend.

"Hudson, Grandma and Grandpa are sleeping," I hear a woman say, then the piano stops.

"Oh, sis, let the kid play." Aiden picks up a dark-haired kid and swings him over his shoulder.

"Uncle Aiden!" the boy screams.

Aiden turns around so I can see the kid's face. "Bulldozer one." He puts the boy down. "Say hello to Saige."

"Hi, Saige," the boy, who can't be more than five, says and runs away.

"Got in late last night?" a woman who has the same dark eyes as Aiden asks and hugs him. "Welcome home, little brother."

"Kendra, this is Saige. Saige, my sister, Kendra."

Kendra steps back from Aiden and smiles, putting out her hand. "Pleasure to meet you."

I can definitely see the age difference between the two of them. She's much older than he is, but she's a good-looking woman and reminds me a lot of his mom.

A scream rings out and Kendra shakes her head, walking away.

"Seriously? Both of you, separate corners." She comes back in with two boys who look just like the boy I just met. Maybe one of them is the boy I just met?

"Bulldozer two and bulldozer three." Aiden points at each of them.

"Triplets?" I ask.

"Identical," Aiden says. "I bet you're scared right now."

A little, because do multiples run in their family? We're far from that point in our relationship, but I can't help that my mind went there.

"Stop it. In vitro. I'm the lucky gal who went in for one and got two more free!" Kendra picks up one of them. "Good thing there's a no return policy." She kisses his stomach.

I slide next to Aiden. "How do you tell them apart?"

"Boys, come here," Aiden yells, and they all do as he says. He points at the first boy. "Hayden?"

"Uncle Aiden." The boy rolls his eyes.

Aiden laughs. Maybe one day I'll get this joke.

"No, it's Hudson, right?" Aiden says.

"Noooo," the boy says.

"Well shit, I guess you're Hunter then."

"Uncle Aiden swore!" the other one yells.

"Tattletale." Aiden scowls.

"Right?" The other boy nods like, 'Can you believe it? He's the enemy.'

"Anyway, let's show Saige how we tell you apart," Aiden says.

"I'm Hayden." The boy models as though he wants me to look at his face, his hair, what's different about him than his brothers.

I see nothing.

"I'm Hunter." The next kid does the same moves as his brother.

For the life of me, I don't see it.

"And I'm Hudson." The third kid doesn't move and stares at me, looking bored.

I get down on my knees and I don't see one difference. All their eye colors are the same. Same haircut. Same everything.

"Okay, give her some help," Aiden says from behind me.

"I'm Hayden and I wear red."

"I'm Hunter and I wear blue."

"I'm Hudson and I wear green."

"Seriously?" I ask Aiden, and he nods.

"Kendra used to put their initials on the bottom of their feet with Sharpies when they were little." He shrugs. "But who knows? Maybe Hudson was really Hayden and Hunter was Hudson at one point."

"Stop it!" Hudson says.

Aiden tickles him. "I'm joking. Most of us don't need the colors anymore. We can tell by your personalities who is who." He leans in. "One day though, they're gonna screw with us."

Aiden walks into the kitchen and I follow. Working in the kitchen is a guy who's definitely the father of the three boys and girl with dark hair and dark eyes.

"Hey, Joe." Aiden shakes his hand. "Joe is our chef for these brunches, and his sous chef is Emma."

Aiden holds out his arms and Emma walks into them. His eyes shut when he hugs her. For a moment, I catch Kendra and Joe sharing a look.

"How's it going?" Aiden asks.

"Good. I made the team," she whispers.

Aiden pulls back and looks at Kendra, who says, "She wanted to tell you herself!"

"Let's go on the ice," Aiden exclaims. "Show me your moves." Emma glances at me and Aiden notices. "Emma, this is Saige, my girlfriend."

"Nice to meet you, Emma." I smile and nod.

"You too."

He ruffles her hair and she quickly fixes it. "After brunch. You and me on the lake."

"She's gonna school you. Her slap shot is deathly." Joe points at his face. It's then I notice a healing black eye.

Aiden cracks up. "What is a chef doing on the ice with the next Hayley Wickenheiser?"

Emma rolls her eyes. Although I don't know the player they're talking about, she must be one of the best.

"Who let these monsters in my house?" Phil shouts from the family room.

Three boys yell, "*Grandpa!*" in unison.

"I'm sure he didn't tell you what you signed up for, did

he?" Kendra whispers in my ear. "Come have some coffee in the sunroom where it's quiet."

I join his sister and find a coffee machine in there.

"I love brunch days. They're the one day I get catered to." She takes a seat and rests her feet on the stool.

"It must be hard with three little ones."

"Emma helps a lot, but as they get older, it gets a little easier. I imagine each phase will bring something different." She sips her coffee. "So tell me about you. My brother doesn't ever tell us much about his personal life, but I heard a bit from Frankie. She said that you're sweet, but you guys aren't actually a couple?"

My face heats. Kendra must be wondering why I'm sleeping with him in his room if we're not together. Time to clear this up. "We weren't when we were in New York, but we are now. It's newish."

"And the whole drink in his face thing?"

I laugh at how absurd it sounds coming from her mouth. "Yeah, he seems to think it makes a difference in how he plays." I shrug.

"So you get to throw white wine in his face before every game?"

I nod.

"Man, I'm jealous." She laughs, and I sip my coffee. "I'd love to be able to have an excuse to do that to my husband."

We both laugh.

"What?" Aiden peeks his head into the sunroom. "Is she telling stories about me?" He slides in next to me on the wicker love seat.

"Not at all," I say.

"Since when are you a superstitious person? He's told you the story of him picking number thirteen, right?" Kendra asks.

"Stop giving all my secrets away," Aiden says good-naturedly.

"He was ten at the time, and until then he'd been number nine, I think."

Aiden nods.

"Then our parents take us to Milwaukee for a night at a hotel where we could swim in a pool and have fun. And he discovers there's no floor thirteen on the elevator buttons. This baffles him, so he keeps asking questions about it the entire trip. We get back, hockey season starts, and he says he'd like number thirteen because he doesn't believe in bad luck."

I look at Aiden and the tips of his ears are pink. He says, "True story. Thirteen ever since."

"That's a great story! And you've had a great career."

"Until he had to have a woman throw wine in his face before every game."

Aiden picks up a magazine and tosses it at Kendra as she laughs.

---

*A*fter brunch, Aiden and Emma go out and skate on the small lake behind the house while the three boys play in the snow with Joe and Phil. Kendra, Barb, and I sit in the sunroom and watch.

"Brunch was great," I say.

"Thanks. Too bad you guys don't live closer," Kendra says. "I could use some babysitters."

Barb and Kendra laugh.

"It must be hard not having Aiden around that much," I say.

Barb nods. "The first few years were bad, but you get

used to it. We raised them to leave the nest. No one wants their adult child living with them."

I understand her point, but still, the love this family has makes me hope I could have it someday. My family isn't terribly close, especially since my parents divorced after I graduated high school.

Emma circles around Aiden. I can tell he's not giving his all, which I find endearing. She scores and raises her hands in victory, doing the same celebration move that Aiden does.

"Oh!" I point.

Kendra laughs. "Yeah, he's kind of her idol."

We keep watching until Aiden eventually calls it quits. He takes off his skates and walks up to the door.

"Maybe she should take your spot on the lineup tomorrow?" Kendra says.

"My skates are old, okay?" Aiden sneers. "Fuck though, Kendra, she's good." He comes in and sits next to me, pressing his cold ear to my cheek.

"I know. Pretty soon she'll be leaving us too."

A look of sorrow hits Aiden. He hasn't told me much about his family. "With her moves, she's definitely gonna have opportunities."

Kendra sips her coffee. "I know."

Silence falls over the room, and Aiden grabs my hand. "Come on, I want to take you on a walk."

"A walk?" Kendra says. "There's the way to a woman's heart. Take her on a walk in negative-ten-degree weather. No wonder you've been single for so long."

I laugh while Aiden scowls at his sister.

"Don't go too far. We have to leave for the bar soon," Barb says.

"I won't, Mom."

After I'm as bundled up as I can be, Aiden and I walk along a path behind their house.

"Do you like it here?" he asks.

"Besides the weather, I do. Your family is great."

"I know." He squeezes my hand.

"They miss you," I say.

"I know."

"Have you ever talked about trying to get traded to Chicago or Minnesota so you could be closer?"

He shrugs. "During the draft, there was some talk about Chicago having an interest in me. My family really hoped it would come together, but it never did. I was pretty homesick my first year, but it's all worked out. Not many of us Drakes have left the town limits. Frankie and I are the only ones. She went off on her own to make a life and I did my thing. I grew up with the goal of making it to the NHL and I've done that. And it's been amazing. But the hardest part was what happened with Emma."

I look at him. "You don't have to tell me."

"I want to. What Frankie said was right. We thought it would be okay, but should've known better. There're a lot of assholes lurking online. Maybe we were naïve. Emma started to get bullied online by people she didn't even know. They'd say nasty things about me, about her. One guy in particular got really vulgar with her and was incessant about it. We didn't know about him until after she tried to end her life."

"What did she do?" I slide my arm through his.

"She took some of Kendra's painkillers she had from when she hurt her back. Luckily Joe was home. He heard her fall. Found the open bottle on her bedside table. I'm not sure what she thought would happen, but they said she didn't take enough to do any permanent damage, thank god. She had a lot of psychiatric help afterward and she seems great now. But yeah, that's why I hate social media. But we should've all been monitoring it better. The fault lies with us."

"How were you afterward?"

He makes a sound. "I hated myself. Blamed myself. But I tracked that guy down, and Maksim and I went to his house and we had words. I ended up beating the shit out of him for doing that to a kid."

"What?" My mouth drops open.

"My family doesn't know," he says, sounding a little ashamed.

"Aiden, I did a search on you. There's nothing out there."

"I settled with the guy out of court. Paid him to keep it quiet."

I stop for a moment, surprised but not. One thing I know for certain about Aiden is that he protects the ones he loves, no matter the cost.

"After that, I was off social media. Nothing good comes from it. Like now, you won't even let me brag to the world about my girlfriend."

I take out my phone and pull off my glove, then log into his account. I pose us in a selfie and we both smile when I snap the picture.

Then I hand him the phone. "Have at it. Say whatever you want."

He smiles and takes off his gloves, then takes my phone, types, and hands it back to me. "Don't read it until I'm on the plane, okay?"

"Why?"

"Just don't."

I smile at him. "Okay."

I close the screen and put the phone in my pocket, then I put my glove back on.

We walk the rest of the trail in silence, enjoying the stillness. I should've known Aiden came from good people. He's so kindhearted himself.

Saige

"Oh, you're not leaving until I see that drink thrown in your face." Kendra comes out from their parents' bar area holding a bottle of white wine.

Aiden rolls his eyes and I laugh.

"He can't go through the airport smelling like alcohol," Barb says, but she's also grabbing a glass.

"I guess we'll have to be careful." Phil grabs a towel and wraps it around Aiden's neck.

Barb fills the glass and sets it in front of me.

"Saige! Saige! Saige!" The triplets pound on the kitchen counter, chanting my name.

Emma stands behind them, smiling. Joe's at work already, and the rest of the family came by to see us off this morning.

I throw the wine all over Aiden. As always, he snakes out his tongue and licks the drops off his lips. Sexiest move ever.

"*Yay!*" the triplets scream.

Aiden takes the towel from around his neck and wipes his face. "You didn't say ready."

"You told me not to last time."

"I like it better when you do it at my house."

I must blush because Kendra says, "Ew, there are children present."

Aiden laughs and picks up his three nephews in two arms. "Be good for your mom."

"Nah," they say.

"I figured. Just don't get arrested."

"Nice." Kendra shakes her head.

He sets them down, giving them each a high five. Then he turns to his parents and hugs each of them, saying goodbye. I swear Barb has tears in her eyes. Kendra pretends she's okay with Aiden leaving, but her deep breath while they're hugging says it's hard for them to watch him go. I can imagine.

"Walk me out," he says to Emma.

The two of them walk out to the garage while I say my goodbyes. The triplets grab glasses and throw water in each other's faces while Kendra scrambles to stop them. Phil goes in as backup.

"Nice meeting you, Saige. Have a safe trip back. You're welcome anytime." Barb picks up my computer bag while I wheel my suitcase. "Take care of him, okay? Maybe show him a life that's not all hockey." Her eyebrows raise as though it will be hard but maybe I can do it.

I smile. "I'll try."

She runs her hand down my back, following me into the garage. Aiden's out there with Emma. The two of them have sticks, him showing her a play.

"Perfect. Damn, you're legit going to beat me soon." He hugs her and whispers something in her ear.

Emma nods a few times, and when they part, she quickly wipes her eyes. The bond they have as uncle and niece is obviously a strong one.

"Okay, Drakes, see you after the season!" He opens up my car door, and I slide in.

As we pull out of the driveway, we wave until they're out of sight.

"I think I love your family," I say.

"I think they love you." He takes my hand. "I can't believe you aren't coming to California with me."

"It's only one night. You'll be back in Florida tomorrow and I'll already be there by the time you arrive. Plus, I'll be watching you."

He nods. "Yeah, and we did the drink thing."

"Yep." I squeeze his hand. "So we're good."

"Yeah." He doesn't sound convinced.

We're driving along when suddenly both our phones go off with notifications.

"What the heck?"

He laughs. "My parents live in the sticks. Service is up and down all the time. Must've been down for a while." I pull my phone out of my purse, but he grabs it. "Not until I'm on the plane."

"But—"

"But nothing. I'll give it to you when you drop me off at the airport."

"So bossy," I say, kind of loving it.

"I expect some sexy pics tonight, okay?"

I chuckle. "I do too."

"You want a dick pic?"

"Sure."

"Okay, careful what you ask for. I might send you Maksim's."

"You want me looking at another man's dick?"

He seems to think a moment. "You're right. What the hell was I thinking?"

Some time later, we pull up to the Milwaukee airport and he parks at departures. I'll keep the rental car until I come back later today to catch my own flight to Florida. He takes his bag from the back.

"Have a great flight and a great game. I'll be watching." I squeeze him tightly in a hug and he kisses the top of my head.

"I'm going to miss you like crazy," he says.

"Me too."

The traffic person blows her whistle at us, so we say one quicker goodbye and he hands me my phone. I smile when he puts it in my hand.

"Don't go running off?" he says.

I get up on my tiptoes. "Never."

We kiss one more time, then he walks through the sliding doors.

The crazy whistle lady blows extra hard and long at me.

"I'm going!" I yell and climb into the rental.

Although I'd love to check my phone, there's no way that lady will let me, so I pull away from the curb, figuring I'll check it when I get to the restaurant where I'm meeting my client.

I park in the lot of the restaurant, happy to be fifteen minutes early. Pulling out my phone, I go to Aiden's Instagram first. As soon as I open the app, I see a bunch of likes and comments, but I go to his profile to find the post before I look at all that.

There we are on his parents' land with snow behind us and our smiling faces pressed to one another's. The caption reads, "Introducing my future wife to the family. No we're not engaged yet, but you know when you know. ;)"

My heart feels as if it's growing and might burst at any moment. Does he really see me as marriage material? We've hardly been dating that long. But even with all that being true, I can't deny I feel the same way.

Ignoring all the comments, I pull up my texts and send him the Kristen Bell GIF with aww and her hands clasped over her heart. He responds with a heart. The man is impossible to read sometimes.

Going back into Instagram, I check a few clients' accounts since I didn't have a great signal at his parents' house. Maksim posted a picture of two hot girls in thongs he saw on the beach. I delete that with the hopes that no one saw it. I swear, I'm this close to locking him out of his own account.

I steel myself as I press on the comments on the picture of Aiden and me. I know there will be some bad ones and I hope I can handle it.

Who is she?

Future wife? WTF

I didn't know he likes the chubby ones.

What's with her lips? She has no upper lip.

He's so dating down.

My chest squeezes painfully. Okay, I knew that would happen. I continue scrolling. Surely there are some positive ones.

Let them be, he's happy. You can see it in his smile.

She's pretty, you're just jelly.

Jealous because it's not you?

Everyone stop judging. We should be happy he found someone.

I thought he was a manwhore?

I've heard he has a reputation. Hope she makes him wear a condom.

I finally click off, unable to read any more. I shake my head and close the app, taking a few deep breaths.

Realizing I can't just sit in my car, I get out and head to the hostess stand to wait for my client. I'd rather wait inside than in my car with the temptation of reading all the nasty comments people leave.

Why is it always easier to believe the bad stuff over the good stuff?

My client picked a sports bar, so when I look up, I see Aiden's name on the ticker at the bottom of the TV screen, talking about how Aiden Drake of the Florida Fury has a girlfriend and his fans are not happy.

Great. I bury my head into a menu and wish I could disappear. I told him this would happen.

I walk into my apartment, drop my bags, and flop down on the couch before turning on the television. After an unexpected layover due to mechanical issues —something you never want to hear when you're about to board a plane—I'm barely home in time to see the end of the game.

I tried to find the AM station in the car but got aggravated when I couldn't find it.

I turn to the channel the game is on and I'm surprised to see that the Fury are losing. From what Aiden said, the team in California isn't very strong. He thought they'd have an easy time beating them.

The announcer comes on over the play. "I have to say, I haven't seen this Aiden on the ice since before the holidays. It's like he can't find his footing on his skates."

Another announcer chimes in. "I'm starting to think the announcement of the new girlfriend has someone distracted. How many times have we seen this before?"

I mute the television. I can't listen to this.

Aiden comes into view. He has the puck, zigzagging between players. A quick glance at the scoreboard tells me that if he scores, he'll tie the game. He shoots the puck, and it ricochets off the top of the net and lands on the stick of the opponent. That player skates away and passes down the ice. Maksim tries to get in the mix, but another guy pushes him into the boards and the guy scores. California wins.

My stomach sinks. I've yet to see Aiden after a loss, much less a game he didn't play well in, and I'm not sure what to expect. It's not like I thought they could go on winning forever, but I did kind of get used to it.

My phone rings right away, Tedi's name flashing on the screen.

"Hey, Tedi," I say.

"They lost. Can you believe it?"

"They were bound to lose at some point. Did you go to California?"

"Nah. Tweetie got his ass handed to him by the coach the other day. Apparently I'm a distraction."

"I guess we're both at fault then."

She laughs. "I wonder how Aiden is gonna be. You threw the drink at him, right?"

I nod, though she can't see me. "Yep."

My eyes remain glued to the screen. Before Aiden can get to the locker room, the press tries to get him on camera. I quickly unmute.

"What can I say? It wasn't our night. We had a few good opportunities to score some goals but couldn't make it happen." He lowers his head and disappears into the locker room.

Okay, he seems like a rational man who can deal with a loss.

Still, maybe I should've gone after my meeting to

support him. But I would've been cutting it close. And I can't follow a man around from city to city my entire life.

"I'm gonna go shower so I'm ready when he calls," I say.

"Okay. See you tomorrow at the office." Tedi hangs up, the both of us sounding depressed.

I shower and get lotioned up, waiting for a call and maybe a sexy FaceTime, but all I get is a text.

Aiden: *Going out with the guys. Blowing off some steam after losing.*

Me: *Okay, be careful. I'm sorry :(*

Aiden: *Thanks. I'll see you tomorrow.*

I stare at his last text. Does that mean I won't hear from him until tomorrow? It sounds like it, which makes me wonder... is this how Aiden deals with a loss? He goes out and gets drunk and forgets he has a girlfriend? I hope not. I've been here before and I'll never go back.

Aiden

*L*osing fucking sucks. On top of losing, all these damn commentators keep saying shit about my new girlfriend. Then Maksim showed me what people are saying about her in the comments of our picture. I'm so over all this shit. I want to just take Saige and run away.

But instead, we have another game tonight and Saige is coming over to throw wine in my face. She said she'd even do it naked like I like to make sure it's extra effective.

I'm out by the pool when she comes to the side gate. She's wearing her bikini with a coverup.

"Strip, woman!" I call.

After going out with the guys, I ended up back in the hotel room early because going out didn't do what it used to for me. I called Saige and we talked until Maksim's drunk ass came back to the room. She made me feel better with her pictures and her teasing. I'm a lucky man, no matter what a bunch of strangers on Instagram say.

She grins. "You first."

"You sure you want to go with that approach?"

She giggles and walks over. "With you? Never." She bends down to kiss me, and I pull her into my lap.

"Want to go skinny dipping?" My hands slide up her torso to grab her breasts.

"Tonight. After you kick some Texas ass," she says.

"I love when you talk dirty." I capture her lips with mine and slide my tongue in. "I missed you so damn much."

One night. One night and I craved her like a junkie looking for his next hit. To have her in my arms right now is pure happiness.

She snuggles up to me on the lounger and my hand dips under the elastic of her bottoms so I can cup her bare ass. We lie there talking about nothing really but basking in each other's company.

Later on, she's naked in the bathroom and I strip down and step in the bathtub.

She shakes her head and drips some wine down the front of herself. "Want to lick it off first?"

She steps into the bathtub with me, and I capture her waist and pull her into me, bending my head to suck on her tit. Just as my tongue is swirling over her nipple and my hand reaches for her other one, the wine splashes on my face. Her chest vibrates with laughter. I run my soaked hair and face between her breasts and her laugh grows deeper.

"I thought I'd surprise you like the first time. Maybe that'll do the trick."

I pick her up and her legs wrap around my waist before I take her to the shower.

I'm in the locker room and there's a bit of a gloom over everyone after losing in California. Even Maksim isn't hanging out in his jockstrap like usual. Most of the rest of the guys have resorted to their old faithful superstitions. Tweetie's eating Taco Bell, Ace didn't wash his socks, and so forth.

Ford sits down next to me, his head in his hands. I don't really want to talk about losing. So what, we lost a game? It happens. Pick yourself up and fucking play with all your heart tonight.

"Looks like I'm the winner," Ford says quietly.

I lean in closer. "What?"

"First one came back as me, but my dad insisted on a DNA test with one of his people too. I'm the dad. I'm gonna be a fucking father."

I blow out a breath. "And what does the mom say?"

"She says nothing right now. I think she wants money."

"And what are you gonna do?"

He stands up with fire in his eyes. I hope he takes that attitude out to the ice with him tonight. "Oh what, you assume I'll do what my dad thinks? Shell out a few mil to get her off my back?"

I hold up my hands because I have no clue what Ford will do.

He points at me. "I'm gonna be a fucking great dad. That's what I'm gonna do. He or she will want for nothing, including a relationship with their father."

I smile and stand, patting him on the back. "That's the Ford I know."

He looks at me with wide eyes. "I'm scared shitless though."

I laugh. "I think you're supposed to be."

"I'm never scared." He shakes his head as though he can't believe it.

"I think it'd be weird if you weren't scared."

He doesn't respond and ventures back to his locker and gets dressed.

My phone dings, so I pull it out.

Saige: *Same seat as the first game. How's my superstitious man doing?*

She's making fun of me, but just like my teammates, I've pulled all the superstitions out of the bag. I had a roast beef sub before the game, had her throw the drink in my face, I got her in the same seat as the first game she saw me.

Me: *Tell me Tedi is next to you*

Saige: *LOL … she is.*

I mean, if we lose tonight and I'm not on my game, it means I'm on my way back into a slump. With only a week until trade deadlines, I might as well pack my fucking bags.

———

*T*he team heads out onto the ice and all I see is Saige on the other side of the glass. I want to hop over the glass and kiss her, but I settle for tapping the end of my stick on the glass and winking instead.

We do our usual warmup skate, and the familiarity of being in our home rink makes me feel as though we'll kick Texas's ass. There's no way we're losing again.

During the first period, we're unstoppable. I've scored two goals with Ford assisting. He's on fire tonight from the adrenaline of finding out he's going to be a dad, I guess. Maksim has helped our goalie keep the puck out of the net multiple times. We're all in rhythm and everything's going great.

In the second, Texas scores, but we're still up by one.

In the third, I get slammed into the boards and all I

can think is that I'm going to have to ask Saige to nurse me back to health with a blow job after the game. I'm not lying, the hit hurt like a motherfucker. Texas ends up stealing the puck after that hit and ties the game.

Revenge being the name of the game in hockey, Maksim slams the guy who slammed me into the boards on the next play and Tweetie shoots me the puck. I skate it down the ice, my eyes on the net, ready to score, but for some stupid reason, I glance at the stands and see Tedi talking to Saige. Saige gets up and walks up the stairs, and I lose my concentration and wonder where she's going. It all happens in a split second. Ford's screaming at me, and I slap shot the puck and it doesn't even come close to the net. That could've been our winning shot.

With little time on the clock, Texas secures the puck and their left winger does some fancy move to get by Maksim, scores, and the clock buzzes at the same time. Texas fucking wins. Unfuckingbelievable.

The minute we're back in the locker room, I pull out my phone and message Saige.

Me: *You okay? I saw you leave.*

Saige: *Yeah, I'm sorry. Restroom.*

I call bullshit because she told me once she held it for an entire game because she didn't want to miss me scoring. I doubt she's that bored with me scoring this early in our relationship.

Me: *I'll be out when I can.*

Saige: *Sorry about the loss. :(*

I hate that fucking sad face emoji.

"*Drake!*" Coach Vittner calls from his office.

All the guys give me the same look. The one that says, "Sorry we lost and you have to bear the wrath since you're captain."

I walk in, already out of my skates and shoulder pads but still unshowered. To my surprise, Gerhardt and Joran are in here. Joran looks up and shakes his head ever so slightly. Is he telling me I fucked up and I'm traded or the opposite? I can't read him.

"Shut the door," Coach says. "Have a seat."

"Two losses, Aiden," is all Mr. Gerhardt says.

Does he know how long our season is? We're not going to win them all. If that was the case, we'd be the Cup winner every damn year.

"I'm sorry. We seem to be off our game."

"Actually, *you* seem to be off your game. I think it's this new girlfriend of yours," Mr. Gerhardt says.

My fists clench at my sides and I narrow my eyes at him. Not him too.

Joran must notice because he steps in and sits at the edge of Coach's desk. "We all want this to work out, Aiden. Carl doesn't want to trade you any more than you want to be traded. But you were on a great roll. Is it a coincidence that after you out your new girlfriend, your game is suffering? I've seen this with a lot of players in new relationships. It's just the distraction of it all. That's why it's better when players meet their girlfriends during the off-season. They spend all their time together and come season start, they're ready for a little space, or ready to part ways altogether." He smiles.

I want to punch his face again. "What are you suggesting?"

"Give each other some space. Let you worry about

winning hockey games, her worry about her social media business, and you two can get back together during the off-season."

I look around the room and see Coach roll his eyes, but Gerhardt looks as if he's actually buying this.

"I've owned this team for so many years, yet I still don't understand guys like you," Gerhardt says. "The world is your oyster, pearls in everyone you open. Why do you only want one oyster when you can have them all?"

I stare blankly at him.

"Have fun with all the oysters you want right now, and when your hockey career is over, find that special oyster you want to hold on to." He pats my leg.

I glance at Coach, who again rolls his eyes.

"By oysters, you mean women?" I ask for clarification.

"Yeah." Mr. Gerhardt seems proud of himself.

"Okay." Joran claps once. "Can I have a moment with Aiden by myself?"

"Here?" Coach asks.

"Where else?" Joran asks.

Coach throws up his hands. "Complete bullshit. You have two minutes, Peters."

Once they leave, Joran sits where Gerhardt was. "Listen, Aiden, Gerhardt isn't bluffing. If you continue to date her and the Fury continue to lose, I'm pretty sure if you're not traded now, you will be at the end of the year. We've been over this. We need you playing well before this next contract negotiation, otherwise we have no leverage. I know you like Saige and she's great, but she manages professional athletes' social media. She understands an athlete's world. I'm sure she'll understand if the two of you need to call it quits until the off-season."

I don't say anything.

"You've known her, what? Almost two months? Hockey

is your life. It's everything you've sweated for for the last twenty-plus years. You're gonna throw that away for some regular pussy for a few months? Come on, Aiden, that's not the guy I know—the guy who works extra hard every practice. The guy who wasn't a shoo-in and scraped and clawed his way to get where he is now. You need to think about what's right for *you*. And speaking strictly as your agent, I think you need to cut her loose for a little bit."

I run my hands down my face. "It's been two games."

"If it was only two games, we wouldn't be here, but you're forgetting the nine games before the revival. Now it's looking like the slump is starting again." He pats me on the back. "It's a hard decision, but all athletes make sacrifices."

He leaves the room and I sit there until Coach barges back in. "Go do your self-reflection bullshit at the yoga studio." He eyes me. "But it would be a good idea for you to get your ass to that psychologist's office."

I stand and leave, happy to see some of the team is already filing out. I send Saige a quick text.

Me: *I'm going to be awhile, I'll call you tonight.*

Without waiting for an answer, I shove my phone back in my locker and head to the showers.

Is there some truth to the suggestion that I'm distracted? Sure, I do think about Saige a lot, and I did miss a good chance at a goal tonight because I was looking at her. But she's the one who brought my game back in the first place.

The water sluices down my back and I stand there for a moment, staring at the floor. I need to think this through. If I end up getting traded to a different city, that'll be the end of Saige and me anyway, so I need to stay on the Fury no matter what it takes.

"Damn it," I mumble and pump some shampoo into my hand.

How do I stay on the team and keep Saige in my life? It doesn't seem like they're both possible at the same time. So maybe I need to do what I can to stay on the team so I can work on being with Saige after I've accomplished the first goal.

Saige

*A*iden has taken this loss a lot worse than the first one. He didn't even call or come over last night. Instead he ended up texting me that he was heading home and going to bed and he'd call me this morning.

So when I'm getting ready for work and there's a knock on my door, I'm surprised to find Aiden in workout clothes at my front step, holding a box of danishes.

"Hey, want to help me get dressed?" I open my towel and flash him.

He doesn't react at all. Instead his face is void of emotion. "Can we talk?"

"What?" I'm a little taken aback at his lack of response, and embarrassed.

"Can I come in?"

I swallow the dryness in my throat and step aside. "Maybe I should get dressed before you break up with me."

He quickly looks away from me. Oh my god, I was half joking, but is that really why he's here?

I stand there and inhale, wetness filling my eyes. "Say what you want and leave."

He heads to my living room and sits on the couch. "Come on. Sit down next to me."

I shake my head. "Say it."

He puts the danishes on the coffee table. Is this what guys do now? Bring the girl some sweets when you're going to break up with her so she can put herself in a sugar coma after you leave? Or better yet, have her gain ten pounds before the next guy?

"Mr. Gerhardt and Joran cornered me last night."

I nod. "And?"

"Saige, please sit down. I want us to come to this decision mutually."

I narrow my eyes as though I didn't hear him right. "Well, Aiden, I don't want to break up, so there is no mutual in this." I wave my hand. "Go ahead and say what you want."

He shakes his head. "I don't want to do this, but it's my career. Everything I've worked for. Everything I know. If I'm not a hockey player, who am I?"

"You're Aiden Drake."

"You know what I mean. I can't jeopardize everything this close to trade deadline. Joran suggested you and I hold off until the off-season to kick things into high gear."

"Joran?" I ask. He's taking relationship advice from a guy like Joran, who doesn't understand the meaning of the word relationship?

"Yeah, and he has a point."

I hold up my hand. "So you're willing to break this off and I'm free to date whoever I want?"

"Well…"

"Yeah, you didn't think that part through, did you? Do you expect me to sit around while you do what you want, then when hockey isn't in the picture, I'm supposed to drop everything and come running?"

He shakes his head. He may play for the Fury, but he doesn't know the meaning of the word. Fury is this feeling

swirling through my veins right now, like I might spontaneously explode if I don't release some of this pent-up
anger.

"You know what? Let me save you the effort. You don't
have to explain. You can leave, and I wish you all the best
with your hockey career. And I do mean that. I hope you
get everything you dreamed of. But once you leave here,
that door is closed. In season, off-season, whenever, it's
closed, and Aiden Drake is barred from entering ever
again."

His dark eyes barely meet mine. "This isn't what I
want."

"No, Aiden, you want everything the way you want it,
all the time. I'm not some toy you pick up and play with
when you feel like, then put back on the shelf when you're
done. I'm a fucking human being."

He walks over to me, his hands out and ready to touch
me. I step back because if he makes contact with me, I'm
going to crumble.

"Just go," I say.

"I'll give you a few days and hopefully you'll see that
this is the right move right now." He turns and pauses at
the door.

The silence is so thick you'd need a chainsaw to cut
through it. For a moment, I wish he'd turn back around
and say he was wrong and he's sorry. But he opens the
door, walks through, and shuts it.

I fall to the floor and bury my head in my hands, finally
allowing the tears free.

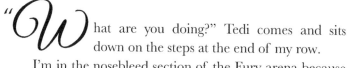

"hat are you doing?" Tedi comes and sits down on the steps at the end of my row.

I'm in the nosebleed section of the Fury arena because I couldn't not come and see if me not throwing a drink in his face made a difference, if everyone was right and I was the distraction in Aiden's game.

"Torturing myself?" I offer her my best guess.

"Saige," she sighs. "Tweetie says Aiden's a mess. That he's screaming and yelling at all the players. He's being more demanding of them and the entire locker room is at odds."

"I don't care. He broke up with me."

She puts her hand on my knee. "And I get that, but why be here then?"

"How did you find me?" I ask.

"I'm your assistant. You bought the ticket online, and they sent it in an email."

"And you're down in the first row?"

She says nothing at first. When Tweetie was told Tedi was a distraction, he didn't break up with her. Because that's what you do when you really care about someone.

"I'll gladly go home with you," she says.

I shake my head.

Tedi stands and I hope she leaves because then I can enjoy my pretzel with extra salt in peace. Instead, she hands two tickets to the guys next to me. "Here. Front row seats. Go."

I shake my head. "Tedi, don't."

"If you're sitting here, so am I."

"Seriously, ma'am?" the guy says.

"Call me ma'am again and I'll rip them up right in front of your face."

They scurry away and she sits down next to me, tears

off a piece of my pretzel, and brushes off some salt. What a waste of salt.

The lights go dark and everyone in the crowd cheers, getting excited knowing the team is about to be introduced. They introduce everyone—Maksim, Ford, the rest of the guys, and when Tweetie is announced, Tedi screams, "That's my man."

"And last, our captain and center, Aiden Drake," the announcer says.

He skates out, raises his stick, and leads his team to skate around the ice before heading to their bench.

Once all the fanfare is over, Aiden comes out in the first period and scores a goal, assisting in another. That seals it. I am the problem.

"It means nothing," Tedi whispers.

A girl in the row in front of us looks at me and whispers to her friend next to her. She thinks she's being sly, but she keeps glancing over her shoulder at me.

Second period, Aiden is everywhere, but the score doesn't change. He steals the puck a bunch of times and gets it down to the net enough, but can't get it past the goaltender.

"Are you her?" the girl in front of me asks.

Tedi twirls her finger at her. "Turn around."

"You are, aren't you?" her friend says.

"Am I who?" I ask.

"Aiden Drake's girlfriend," the first girl asks. "I recognize you from the pictures."

"You should be in the first row, or is he hiding you?" the other says.

"Why would he hide her?" Tedi asks. "Mind your business and turn around."

"We're not together anymore," I admit, and Tedi sighs.

"For now. It'll change," Tedi tells them. "So keep your clothes on."

I give Tedi a pleading look and she stops.

During the third period, I get up to leave after Aiden scores.

"Come on, you cannot believe in all this bullshit." Tedi follows me.

I head into the bathroom. As luck would have it, those two girls are in there, putting on their lipstick. Probably so they can go wait with the other women for Aiden and his teammates after the game.

"Did you break up because of the Instagram post?" one of the girls asks.

The other girl shhs her, but I stop before going into a stall. "No."

"Because if you did, I was going to say those people are just jealous and you shouldn't let random people who hide behind a screen ruin something for you."

"I had the same view until I read those things about myself. It makes it hard."

The girl nods. "I know."

I stare at Tedi. *See? Not every woman wants our men.* "But we broke up because of something else."

"I'm sorry," she says.

"Thank you."

I look at Tedi. "Take me home."

She puts her arm around my shoulders. "I'm the best date ever, you just wait. I'll stop at any fast-food place you want, and I'll let you watch whatever movie you want while I trash talk your ex."

I laugh and leave the Fury arena for the last time. This isn't me. I don't sit here and feel sorry for myself. Screw Aiden Drake. He's the one who lost out this time.

Aiden

*W*e won, even though not one drop of wine hit my face before the game. The Fury won with me scoring one goal and one assist. As good as it feels knowing I'm performing again and there's just one more game left before trade deadline, I've been grumpy and mean and an asshole since I split with Saige. I want her in my life, but getting traded won't accomplish that anyway. And if being with her is the distraction that causes a trade to happen, then how do I handle this double-edged sword without either of us getting hurt?

Lucky for me, Ford flies me and Maksim up to New York and we catch a game there. Being with my friends is a welcome distraction. I love playing hockey, but I love watching it too, especially when you have friends who came up with you on the ice.

We opted for front row seats obviously, but just to infuriate our friends playing, we're wearing our own jerseys.

"So that's it? You ended it?" Ford asks.

"I don't wanna talk about it."

"You're being a complete pussy," Maksim chimes in before taking a swig of his beer.

"We won, didn't we? I guess the white wine didn't have anything to do with it to begin with."

They're both quiet and look at one another. Maksim shakes his head at Ford.

"What?" I ask.

"Nothing," Maksim says.

Ford stands. "Go. Go!" He pounds on the glass when Jake, a guy who used to play with us, skates toward the goal and scores. "Woo-hoo!"

Jake comes over and pounds on the glass when he sees us.

"The best thing to happen to him was moving away from you three." Jake's wife, Bree, comes over with a baby on her hip.

"Who's this little one?" Ford touches the little guy's hand.

"This is Jake Jr."

"You know you miss Florida," I say.

Jake and Bree are the couple from high school who made it. They've been together since I've known Jake and they have two daughters, along with this little man.

"You came down from your suite to see us?" Maksim says. "I feel honored."

"Well, you three in your Fury jerseys stick out in this crowd. Not to mention my lunatic husband keeps giving you attention every time he's down on this end."

We all laugh.

Jake skates by us again and he's got the puck now. We all cheer for him, ready to celebrate another goal, but another player comes at him from behind and runs him into the boards. Jake loses his footing and crashes headfirst. The energy in the arena shifts and silence commences when Jake doesn't get up. I glance at Bree and see that her face is ghost-white.

"Get up, Jake," she whispers. "Come on, baby, get up."

The more she talks, the more I hear the emotion in her

tone. As if on cue, Jake Jr. starts crying, as if he feels the tension filling his mom's body.

I hold out my hands. "Give him to me. Go."

She hands me the baby and runs over to the bench. The coach lets her climb over as the team doctor goes to Jake on the ice.

This is what we all fear. That one play will take you out when you think you have it all. We're all invincible until it happens.

"Fuck," Ford says when Jake still doesn't get up.

All the players kneel on the ice, and the stretcher comes out after the team doctor waves them over. Jake isn't moving a muscle, his body still limp on the ice.

A woman comes down the aisle with Bree and Jake's two girls. Bree points at us, and I hand over Jake Jr. How can she be dealing with this and still be thinking of what needs to happen with the kids?

"Thank you," the woman says when she takes the baby.

A man hands Bree her purse and the woman screams to Bree, "We'll meet you at home."

I watch Jake get carted off the ice on the stretcher toward Bree. She whispers something to him and kisses his forehead. The crowd claps as they disappear through the opening toward the locker room, and I swallow the bile in my throat.

Sitting down, I catch my breath as the players return to the ice. Surely the player who hit him from behind is gonna get his ass nailed to the boards after he gets out of the penalty box. But as I watch, I'm struck by how the play goes on. Not that I'm not used to it. I'm just usually involved in the play, having to move on from what happened and concentrate on the present. Nobody is saying let's call it a night. These fans might care what happens to Jake, but it doesn't stop them from enjoying the rest of the game.

The only people whose world just crashed and burned were Jake, Bree, and their little ones. If it was me, it would only be me. I'd be carted off by myself, wake up in the hospital by myself. Sure, maybe my family would come down, but for how long? They have their own lives.

The more I wrap my head around it, the more a sick feeling sours my stomach. I've made the worst mistake of my life. "I have to go."

"We can head out," Ford stands.

"I need to go home," I say.

"Why?"

"Because I need to win Saige back."

Maksim smiles at Ford. "Now you can tell him."

"What?"

"She was at our last game. Tweetie said she and Tedi were in the nosebleeds, watching you through the first and second period." Ford claps me on the back. "She's your lucky charm, man. Not the wine. Saige."

I huff and jog up the stairs.

"You need to do something big to win her back," Ford says from behind me. "Good thing I'm your best friend."

"I'm his best friend," Maksim says.

"I am," Ford argues.

I turn and look at them over my shoulder. "You both are, okay?"

"Who's gonna be your best man then?" Ford asks. "I should add that we all know how good I look in a tuxedo."

I shake my head. "Let me win her back first."

*O*ne night later…

*I*t took a lot of brainstorming between the three of us on the plane home to figure out what I needed to do to try to win Saige back after my epic fuckup. Bree messaged us to let us know that Jake would be okay after a few weeks' rest for a concussion. Knowing he'd make a full recovery set us all at ease.

I'm sorry for what happened to him, but at the end of the day, I'm grateful because it allowed me to see that the most important thing in your life is who you have in it. And I want Saige in my life, no matter what. Whether I'm playing the best I ever have or like complete shit, I want her there to see me through it all.

I read back over what I wrote, then exhale a deep breath and press Post.

This is Aiden Drake. Not my social media manager. I've locked her out so she can see the post but not change it. I'm a lot of things to a lot of people. I'm a son, a brother, an uncle, a teammate, a captain, and yes, the center of the Florida Fury. But the role I valued the most was being Saige's boyfriend. I despise social media, but the woman I love makes a living off of it, which is why I'm doing this here. I fucked up and put my career before the woman I love. I'm sorry, Saige. I plead temporary insanity because from the minute I saw you at that party, I knew you were her. The woman I've been waiting for. I waited until you were available, then I shamelessly threw you to the side. I know now that there is no such thing as superstition, but I do believe in fate or destiny. I was with you on the first second of this year and I want to be with you on the last second of my time here on this earth. If you think you can forgive me, there's a ticket at will call for you, but there's one hitch. You have to sit in the wives/girlfriends area because that's where you belong. I hope to see you tonight.

CHAPTER 32

"Every day for the rest of my life."

Saige

I get the Instagram notification that the password on Aiden's account has been changed, and after I read what he wrote, I try right away to get back into his account to delete it. I try to guess the password, trying all different combinations, but nothing works. Damn him.

"Come on, let's get going," Tedi says, waiting for me at the door of our office.

"I'm not sure if I'm going."

"No, we're not playing that game. Get in the car." She opens the door.

"What game?" I stay seated.

"You love him. He apologized within only a few days. Now go and allow him to woo you." Tedi waves her hand again.

"I'm not gonna let him woo me after what he did."

She lets the door shut and stares blankly at me. "Why not?"

"Because he humiliated me."

Tedi juts out a hip. "So this is about your pride?"

"Stop looking so annoyed with me."

"Listen, Saige, I've known you a long time. And eventually you're going to go there and sit in the wives and girlfriend section because you love the man and he loves you. So either we drag it out or we just go now. There's nothing wrong with forgiving him easily."

"Ugh, you aggravate me." I stand and grab my sweatshirt.

"Only because you know I'm right."

I walk by her, and we get in her car and drive over to the arena.

"If Tweetie didn't leave me a ticket next to yours, he's in so much trouble," Tedi says as we approach will call.

Lucky for Tweetie, he did, and we both head inside the arena. The game is already in the first period by the time we show up. I hope we can slide in unnoticed. But as soon as I sit down, the other wives and girlfriends all smile my way, obviously fans of Aiden Drake.

"Holy shit." Tedi elbows me. "You're on the Jumbotron."

I hate that thing. Everyone cheers when they see me, and Aiden and his teammates look around. Somehow, Aiden's eyes go directly to mine. He smiles and my heart thumps. Then there's a line change and he goes to the bench.

Except Aiden goes past the bench. The camera guy follows him while we all watch on the Jumbotron.

"What is he doing?" I ask.

"He's making it up to you. Relish it," Tedi says as everyone intently watches the Jumbotron. I don't know if anyone is even watching the game at this point.

Aiden's walking through hallways to the locker room, takes off his skates in what must be record time, and puts on a pair of slides. Then he sets off in a run and "I'm Gonna Be (500 miles)" by the Proclaimers plays as he runs, the camera shaking behind him the entire time.

He goes through more tunnels, then comes out at the entrance to the arena, but he looks up and realizes he's in the wrong section. The crowd laughs, and he goes back through the opening. He comes out in two more wrong sections and the crowd thinks it's hilarious, but I just want him next to me. The wait feels excruciating.

I watch the camera intently, and when he pops on screen again, he's holding flowers, chocolates, and a big teddy bear wearing a shirt with the number thirteen on it. I sigh, but I search all over for him, unable to see where he is in the arena. Then he taps me on the shoulder, and I turn to see him.

My breath catches in my throat. "Hi."

"Flowers, candy, a teddy bear, and…" He looks for a place to set them down and the woman behind him takes them. "My jersey?"

He holds it up, and I raise my hands so he can put it over my head.

"I was a complete asshole, and I promise you, it will never happen again. If I don't have you, none of the rest of it even matters." He takes my face in his hands. "*You* are my life. Hockey is just what I do."

"Kiss me," I say.

"Every day for the rest of my life." He places his lips on mine, and all the issues we've had to get to this point fade away.

Deep down, I knew it the first night too—this is where we need to be. Once he closes the kiss, the crowd roars and we look over to see that we're on the Kiss Cam.

"Log into your account." I hand him my phone.

"Why?"

"Just do it." He only ever went back onto social media to get me to stick around and I'm not going anywhere now, so this is the least I can do for him.

He types in his password and logs in… then I press *Delete Account.*

There is no user ID AidenDrake13

Aiden

"So I finally got you into the therapist chair," Paisley, the Florida Fury psychologist, says when I sit down.

"Yeah, but I don't really need any help. I don't wanna brag, but I kind of figured out my shit all by myself."

"Is that so?" she asks, jotting something in her notepad.

"Yep. Don't you watch ESPN?"

"Oh, are we talking about your public declaration of love?"

"I suppose you have to keep up with hockey and stuff if you're going to try figuring us out." I tap my temple. I lie down on the couch because after the night I had with Saige, I got no sleep. She's insatiable and I love her for it. "Actually, I do have one question, doc. Do you think there's a time when it's too early to ask someone to move in with you?"

"Do you want to ask Saige to move in with you?"

I laugh. "Well, a moving van is showing up at her place right about now."

It's been two weeks and I'm still on a winning streak. We may not make the Cup, but we have the points to make the playoffs. Regardless, I'm done waiting. I want Saige with me all the time.

"And you never told her or even asked her?" Paisley asks.

"Well, no. I should have, right? Probably."

She taps her pen on the paper. "You know what I find amazing with all you hockey players? You think you can just do whatever and suffer the consequences later."

"We're professional athletes. Plus, I know Saige wants to live with me. She barely goes home. I thought I was romantic, sending a truck to surprise her."

"And the fact she now has to pack all her stuff without warning?"

She's clearly a woman, thinking of all these issues.

"They'll pack for her. All she has to do is drive over to my house." My phone vibrates in my pocket. "Should I answer? It's probably her. We'll put her on speaker." Before waiting for a response, I answer and smile, seeing her name on the screen. "Hey, babe."

"Don't babe me. Why is there a moving company here?"

"They're going to take your stuff to my house."

"Aiden," she says in that tone I know will make her a great mom to our kids someday. "We didn't discuss this."

"Do you not want to move in with me?" I ask. "By the way, Paisley is here if you have any concerns."

"Paisley? Aiden, what the hell is going on?"

"Oh no, Paisley's the team psychologist. She thinks I should've asked too."

"Glad to see someone there has brains. God knows your locker room is just full of egos."

I laugh because my girl is funny. "So you're packing up? I'll meet you at home?"

She sighs and says nothing for a second. "Yes."

"See, I knew she'd say yes. Okay, babe, we're just wrapping up. I'll be at home waiting for you." I cup my hand over the phone. "Naked in the hot tub."

Paisley rolls her eyes.

"Bye, Paisley. Good luck with the job," Saige says with a laugh.

"Thanks, I need it."

I hang up with my girl. "See? I'm great. My life is fantastic."

"Well…" Paisley says.

"So I'm gonna go." I stand from the couch.

"We still have forty-five minutes," she says, eyeing her watch.

"I hate to waste time. Plus, I told the next guy his time is now."

She looks baffled.

"Maksim Petrov."

"You got him here?" she asks. "Impressive. I've been working on the two of you."

"I was really busy winning my girl back. See you later, nice talking to you." I stand and leave, keeping the door open for Maksim, who's waiting.

Getting him here took some heavy bribing, but I made him a bet and he lost. That's the one thing hockey players don't renege on. If you lose the bet, you do the time.

Maksim blows out a breath and sits on the couch, looking irritated.

"Have fun, you two," I say with a wave.

"I'll be here, but I'm not talking," Maksim says as I shut the door.

Poor Paisley's in for a boring hour.

I rush out of her office and into my SUV because I'd rather be home with my girl on the first day of us living together forever.

The End

Cockamamie Unicorn Ramblings

This is our second crack at a sports romance series. In the first one we wrote snowboarders, and the stories were much shorter. We decided we wanted to write sports romance since a lot of our readers were asking us to and knew we wanted to write either football or hockey. After a poll in our reader group, Piper Rayne's Unicorns, it was close, but hockey won out. This posed some problems. One being that neither one of us knows a ton about hockey. Not even Piper and she's from Canada. I mean we can appreciate the suits as the players come into the arena, the chiseled abs under the jersey, and follow along with the game but that's about it. Thankfully, her husband does and was at our beck and call for any questions we had about ways to describe the game in a way that we didn't sound like complete amateurs. I mean feelings, humor, love story we got covered, but play by plays in hockey, um... not so much.

So, once we knew we had Piper's husband on board, we set up to write our first book. We purposely wrote a prequel to go in an anthology in January with the first three guys from Florida Fury, so we knew where Aiden and Saige's story was going. We had to put the final touches on but not much came as a surprise to us. Maybe this means we're actually evolving into the authors who have their shit together. Probably not. Lol.

Rayne loved writing sports romance again. Athletes are her go to one-click keyword and she fell hard for this new world we're writing. So much so, she might just push for us to write a lot more than the Hockey Hotties. In our true nature, family is always at our core of our stories and if you've read The Baileys or The Greenes, we hope you'll see that the Florida Fury are no different. The team is a family, just a found family.

We hope you fell in love with our guys. Each one brings something different to the table. Book boyfriends for every-body! :P

Without our team you wouldn't have any of our books! Seriously, they take on a lot of the work off our hands so that we can write!

Danielle Sanchez and the entire Wildfire Marketing Solutions team.

Cassie from Joy Editing for line edits.

Ellie from My Brother's Editor for line edits.

My Brother's Editor for proofreading.

Hang Le for the cover and branding for the entire series. Love! (Wait until you see the rest. *swoon*)

The Cover Lab for supplying the vision of Aiden for us.

Bloggers who consistently carve out time to read, review and/or promote us.

Piper Rayne Unicorns who love our characters like as much as we do!

Readers who took the time to read our story when there's so many choices out there.

Maksim is next and we cannot wait to unfold his layers—and his Russian curse words. You just know there's something behind this tough Russian who keeps everything sheltered inside. We'll be sitting there right next to Paisley as she uses her therapist techniques to get him to open up!

Xo

Piper & Rayne

About the Author

Piper Rayne is a USA Today Bestselling Author duo who write "heartwarming humor with a side of sizzle" about families, whether that be blood or found. They both have e-readers full of one-clickable books, they're married to husbands who drive them to drink, and they're both chauffeurs to their kids. Most of all, they love hot heroes and quirky heroines who make them laugh, and they hope you do, too!

Also by Piper Rayne

Hockey Hotties

My Lucky #13

The Trouble with #9

Faking it with #41

The Greenes

My Beautiful Neighbor

My Almost Ex

My Vegas Groom

The Greene Family Summer Bash

My Sister's Flirty Friend

My Unexpected Surprise

My Famous Frenemy

The Baileys

Lessons from a One-Night Stand

Advice from a Jilted Bride

Birth of a Baby Daddy

Operation Bailey Wedding (Novella)

Falling for My Brother's Best Friend

Demise of a Self-Centered Playboy

Confessions of a Naughty Nanny

Operation Bailey Babies (Novella)

Secrets of the World's Worst Matchmaker

Winning My Best Friend's Girl

Rules for Dating your Ex

Operation Bailey Birthday (Novella)

The Modern Love World

Charmed by the Bartender

Hooked by the Boxer

Mad about the Banker

The Single Dad's Club

Real Deal

Dirty Talker

Sexy Beast

Hollywood Hearts

Mister Mom

Animal Attraction

Domestic Bliss

Bedroom Games

Cold as Ice

On Thin Ice

Break the Ice

Box Set

Charity Case

Manic Monday

Afternoon Delight

Happy Hour